Just a Girl in the Whirl

Books by Annie Wood

Dandy Day
A Quantum Love Adventure
Just a Girl in the Whirl

Just a Girl in the Whirl

Annie Wood

SPEAKING VOLUMES, LLC
NAPLES, FLORIDA
2021

Just a Girl in the Whirl

Cover artwork by Annie Wood

ISBN 978-1-64540-447-7

Acknowledgments

Thank you, Pops, my playwright father. I know you have something to do with this writing thing in me. I am grateful for that and so much more that stems from you.

Thank you my talented and supportive husband, Peter Arpesella. Your belief in me means more than I can say. Ti amo. Grazie mille. And thank you to the memory of my brother, Miram, who was funny and sweet but also an addict. He inspired the father character in this story. And to my beautiful Ema, your lasting love continues to fill me up. Toda arba. And thank you, dear reader, for without you, my stories would possibly remain in my head and it gets way too noisy in there as it is.

Thank you. Thank you. Thank you.

i carry your heart with me (i carry it in my heart) i am
never without it (anywhere i go you go, my dear; and
whatever is done by only me is your doing, my darling)

—e.e. cummings

It takes courage to grow up and become who you really are.

—e.e. cummings

brood

{brood}
a family of offspring or young.

In the past 747 days I've made my 747th breakfasts for my family. I barely have to think about what I'm doing anymore, the eggs just poach themselves. Doing the same thing, day in and day out, gives my life the feeling of being stuck in slo-mo. In fact, I'm moving so freakin' slowly I may as well be standing still. It's like I managed to step into a vat of cement while everyone around me is coasting along on one of those people movers they have at the airports. Also, my particular vat of cement happens to be on a carousel, going around and around and around. So, sure, there's movement, only I'm not getting anywhere.

"Damn it." I bend down to pick up yet another broken glass. My bad. As usual. When my mind wanders, it takes my coordination with it.

"Lauren. Don't say damn," my kid sis reprimands.

"You're right, Sara. Sorry. Finish your scrambled eggs, okay?"

"Okay."

"Ouch." I cut my pinkie on a sliver of broken glass.

We're out of Band-Aids," Matty informs. "You should get more."

Gee, thanks, sis. Don't bother getting up."

"I won't," she tells me as she continues scarfing down the food I made her.

Yep, this is my brood. Not on purpose, though. I mean, I didn't plan this brood or birth this brood, it just sort of turned out that they're now, mostly mine.

My eighteenth birthday is in 99.3105497 days away and then I'll be free. At least, that's how it should work. But, in all actuality I will most likely remain so very much—not free. Sure, free from high school, lame dances, excessive homework, and mean kids with inferiority complexes—hallelujah for all that. But as it turns out, there is oh so much more to be free from.

I might have unreasonably high hopes for the magic age of eighteen. It probably won't feel that different, seeing that I've been adulting ever since my dad bailed on us two years ago. Still, as soon as I'm a legit adult, I have a plan. I plan on attending The Write Stuff writing fellowship in Santa Barbara. Not that I've actually been accepted. Okay, not that I've actually applied. But if I did actually apply and if I were to actually be accepted, as an actual adult, I'd be able to actually attend. I bookmarked the website and started filling out the application, but then got sidetracked by my family suddenly imploding and I stopped thinking about my future entirely. The Now needs my attention. There was really no choice in the matter because The Now began to scream at me at the top of its lungs, claiming that it needed me to stay home and take care of things. The Now can be ear-piercingly loud. The Now can be super bratty and extremely demanding. So, when the now hollered at me, I caved in and listened.

Still, thoughts of my potential freedom pop up all the time. What it must feel like to be away from home and doing what you love. I want to attend this writing fellowship so badly I can practically taste it. It tastes sweet like raspberry jam and fresh seaside air. I imagine I'd be able to breathe better in Santa Barbara because it's near the ocean and far from home. In fact, it may not be a simple want at this point; this feeling might have advanced from want to need. I need to go there like I need oxygen. Because if I don't go, if I'm still in this hectic house, in this hot, lonely San Fernando Valley by the time this summer is over, my feet could very well be stuck in cement going 'round and 'round on this carousel indefinitely. My own personal *Groundhog Day*.

Fixing & wishing:

Fixing the house + fixing my sisters + fixing my mom + wishing my dad would come back = certain madness.

99.3105497 days.

***

"It needs more salt." Matty thrusts her breakfast plate at me as I work feverishly to cook up everyone's eggs, special order, just the way each of them have grown accustomed. I want to argue with my sister that too much salt isn't good for her, but she'll only argue back that she's not a middle-aged man with high cholesterol. Sometimes it can be annoying how smart my tweeny sis is. I grab the sea salt and give a few quick shakes on top of her two eggs scrambled with diced chives and a sprinkle of thyme. Also, just for the record, it SO does NOT need more salt. This dish is spiced to perfection. She knows it irks me when she asks for more of anything without even trying it first.

She takes the plate without so much as a "thanks" and goes over to sit next to Sara, who says, "I need more juice." Then she smiles that sweet little toddler smile of hers and adds, "pweese."

Of course, she gets what she wants. She often does. The thing is, I really want both of them to get what they want because that sort of thing—getting what you want—doesn't always come easy for us Brightons.

Our family may be broken, but our breakfasts don't have to be.

After Dad left, I'm guessing in an effort to create a new identity, Matty chopped off most of her hair, dyed it purple, and started wearing it all spiky. It sounds nuts, but it doesn't look half bad with her new nose piercing and the press-on tattoos that she's "auditioning" for the real thing. All of this would be fine if it wasn't such an obvious reaction to someone else's action. She used to be upbeat and bright, but after Dad left she got pissed. Still bright, but these days her fingers rest firmly on the dimmer switch. She's taken up arguing as her new hobby. If you tell her you like the Pacific Ocean, she'll tell you that the Atlantic Ocean is way better (even though she's never been). If you complain about the humidity, she'll tell you how much she loves the humidity. Seriously, who loves the humidity? Matty says she hates Dad's guts and she doesn't miss him at all. Of course, neither are true. She does have one cool party trick, though. If you say, "Tell me something I don't know." She will. And it'll be something you really don't know and it'll be true. She likes to act like it annoys her when you ask, but we all know that it makes her feel special.

"Shoot." I spill grilled potatoes on me as I attempt to transfer them onto the plate I'm making for Mom. I catch my reflection in the kitchen window and I have the urge to reach out and help the girl staring back at me. Or at least give her a proper hair cut.

I haven't had so much as a trim in two years and I've given up on makeup all together. I still shower, so all is not lost. I shower for exactly two minutes and thirty-four seconds. Not because California's in a major drought right now (we are), but because two minutes and thirty-four seconds is exactly the amount of time needed to get all of the important bits clean on non-hair-washing days. Being shower efficient leaves me enough time to make this breakfast for my sisters, take them wherever they need to go, make sure Mom eats something and also do the laundry, clean the dishes, and maybe, at some point today, brush my teeth and put on some clean clothes.

The TV is blaring from the living room. A commercial about a talking rabbit robot toy.

"I need that!" Sara yells at the TV.

"You don't need that!" I yell back, making my way into the living room to shut it off.

"Hey. I was watching."

"No TV right now. Finish your breakfast in the kitchen, please."

Sara starts to cry as I lift her up to bring her back to the kitchen. Her cries are super high-pitched and almost always right into my ear. I think when you leave the hospital with a newborn, they should also give you a lifetime supply of earplugs. Seems like the right thing to do.

I place Sara back in her chair at the table and bring her an animal cracker.

"Elephant." she happily exclaims, taking the cookie.

We fostered a puppy once when I was around ten and whenever he did something right, something that we wanted him to do, we gave him a cookie. That's the way to go with Sara. Maybe taking child rearing education from my puppy experience doesn't exactly make me mother of the year, but I'm also not exactly a mother.

The doorbell rings. My hands are full, so I look over at Matty for some help.

"Matty?"

She looks up at me, clueless. "What?"

I dry my hands and answer the door.

A girl, a little older than me, stands there smiling. She has a book in her hands.

"Hi. I'm Carolina. How are you today?" "Fine, thanks."

"Great. I'm in your neighborhood today discussing the Bible."

"Oh, we're not really Bible people."

"I understand," she says. But she doesn't go away. She just smiles and continues with her pitch. "With all of the terrible recent events in our world today, you may wonder if God really exists. And if he does exist, does he care at all about the human race? What do you think?"

Whoa. Heavy stuff for eight o'clock in the morning.

"Umm...well, I'm not sure. I mean, I think that if there is a God, maybe he's feeling a bit overwhelmed these days?"

Carolina giggles a little and her speech relaxes. "Yeah, probably. I often find comfort in an encouraging scripture in the Bible where God explains how he's going to step in and right all of the wrongs in the world. Here." She hands me the book and points to a passage. "Would you like to read this out loud? Revelations 21:3-4.

I look behind me, wondering if I left the stove on or if Matty's eating all of Sara's leftovers, or if Sara found her way to the cookie jar, or if Mom's plate is getting cold before we even have a chance to get it to her. But I also don't want to be rude. This girl is just doing her job. Wait, is this a job? Anyway, the sooner I read what she wants me to, the sooner I can shut the door without feeling like a total jerk.

I read the passage out loud, quickly, *The earth attains its celestial glory and God shall wipe away all tears from their eyes; and there shall be no more death, neither sorrow, nor crying, neither shall there be any more pain: for the former things are passed away.*

"I hand the book back to her. "That's nice. I think."

"Do you find that encouraging?" Carolina asks.

"I don't know. I guess, if it actually happened, if someone magically took away all the pain in the world, then, yeah, sure, I'd find it encouraging."

Carolina looks surprised. There's a dejected look on her face.

Since I'm pretty sure I'm the cause of her facial contortion, I add, "But...I do like the language. It reminds me of a poem. Shakespeare or something."

She asks me if it's okay if she stops by another time and I sort of agree to it, then as slowly and as politely as possible, I close the door.

I head back into the kitchen, but now I can't stop thinking about God. If there is one, what does he look like? Is he a he? Maybe she's a she? Maybe neither. Maybe God isn't like a person at all, but more like a superhero. That would explain why he/she is invisible. At least to me. At least so far. But I'll keep my eyes open, just in case I run into him/her.

"Here." I hand Matty Mom's plate.

"Why can't you take it to her?"

"She likes to see you."

"Right. If she even looks up."

"Just go." I push her toward the stairs.

I've only been on this planet for seventeen years, nine months, and eight days, and I'm already exhausted. But I hate complaining. It's so whiny. I'm really fine. It's all fine. My family is fine. Everything is fine. It's been one thousand, ninety-seven days and twelve hours since Richard left and I have everything completely, totally, utterly handled.

relinquish

{ri-ling-kwish}
to renounce or surrender to let go; release:
to relinquish one's hold.

"I never know what to say to her." Matty complains.

"You don't need to say anything. Just your presence is enough."

I put Sara's old baby monitor in Mom's room so I can hear Matty enter. I imagine Mom is watching TV with it turned off again.

"This is my favorite part," Mom says.

Matty doesn't say anything. She's probably just staring at her. Matty often just stares at her.

"Tell me something I don't know," Mom says.

After a moment, Matty says, "Did you know that Americans watch two hundred and fifty billion hours of television a year?"

I can hear Mom applauding and then saying softly, "I love you so much, Matty."

Matty says nothing in response. I could almost hear her heart break into a million little pieces, then I hear footsteps, and then the door closing. Matty comes zooming down the stairs. She pauses and looks out the front window. "Grandma Gayle is here."

Grandma Gayle is Dad's mom and when she knocks on the door, it means one thing and one thing only: *it's payday.*

I open the door. She stands there, studying me. I know I look like a hot mess with my wild, unbrushed hair and olive oil stained t-shirt. I'm the polar opposite of this woman who stands before me. Gayle is tall, super thin, and doesn't look like anybody's grandma. Not at all. She speaks abruptly, using as few words as possible so she can get to the point quickly. I'm pretty sure she uses less words than most mortals.

"She out of bed?" she asks.

"She's fine," I answer.

"The children?" she asks.

"They're fine," I answer.

She hands me a check.

I take it. "Thanks."

I've heard stories from my friends about their brownie-baking grannies and how much their grand-mas spoil and love them. Must be nice. But, that's just not in the cards for us Brightons. The main reason for that is—Grandma Gayle never much cared for Mom.

She thought her son, (you know, the one who abandoned his family) could do much better. Oh-kaaaay.

"Anything else?" she asks as she turns to leave. "I've got it handled," I tell her.

That's what I always tell her. Honestly, I wouldn't even take the money if we didn't need it to pay the mortgage. And to eat. I'll continue to take the money and keep everyone alive and in one piece until my parent's get their crap together.

Preferably within the next 99.3105497 days.

dream to cry

It's night.
I'm sleeping.
I'm dreaming.

Dream Lauren is busy writing from up top her favorite tree.

She looks down and winks at me. Real Me would never wink. Bad guys in movies wink. Still, this dream version of myself winks and it wouldn't matter to her whether Real Me approves. Dream Lauren is not bothered by what other people think of her. Even if that other people is just another version of her.

In every dream, Dream Lauren drops down pages from her journal, and in every dream, I stand below with my arms outstretched, always ready to catch them as they float down.

She feels it build up inside her,
an inner quake setting off a tsunami that will
destroy
everything
in

its path.
a rise in the belly,
coming in tidal waves.
A tickle in the nose,
that isn't an oncoming sneeze.
She trained herself to ignore,
to respond quickly.
She puts up sandbags to keep it away.
her smile is her glass wall.
She can't afford a crack in the surface.
She's gotten so good at pretending.
She can feign indifference with the best of them.

I wake up and grab my journal, and make a beeline for the bathroom in order to write it all down before I forget.

dick

It's breakfast number 748 and Sara comes blasting into the kitchen, holding up her pink, glittery tutu.

"I want to wear this."

"You've worn that five days in a row."

"Sooooo?"

"So, people will think you don't have any real clothes."

"This is real."

Sensing a tantrum coming on and due to lack of sleep and total exhaustion, I let her wear the damn tutu.

Ever since actor-addict-father bailed on us twenty-four months ago to do summer stock (and his co-star), I've been the captain of this ship called life. I guess we're all captains of our lives, but usually we're not asked to take the helm solo and venture onto the high seas in stormy weather until we're full-fledged adults. For the past two years, I've been hoping that one of the actual adults in my life would reclaim the role of captain, so I could jump ship and swim to safety. Or maybe just splash around a bit, for, you know, *fun*.

But that hasn't happened yet.

Placing the breakfast bowls in front of my sisters, I make sure to sprinkle a little cinnamon on top of the oatmeal because it adds dimension and color. Visuals matter. Well, at least to me.

"I need a new pair of jeans," Matty says scooping large spoonfuls into her mouth.

"You have enough jeans."

Sara then breaks into song, *"It's a hard knock life, for us...It's a hard knock knock . . ."*

"Sara, don't sing with your mouth full."

Matty thrusts her iPhone up to my face, showing me an Instagram post of a pink haired teen in ripped jeans. "I don't have these specific jeans. Look how cool."

"You can turn one of the jeans you already have into that with a pair of scissors."

"OMG, when did you get so old, bossy-butt?" she grumbles.

Ignoring her, I continue making breakfast, wondering if my sister thinks that I have secret access to some sort of hedge fund or something.

When we all refer to our dad now, we call him by his first name, "Richard." Except for Matty. Matty prefers calling him by the popular, (and appropriate) nickname for Richard, *Dick.* The good news about Matty is that she usually listens to me, more or less. I suspect that the real Matty, deep down inside, actually knows that I can see her. Like, really see her. She knows that I know that she's not the rough and tough kid that she's pretending to be.

Sara is four years old, so she was only two when our lives imploded. She doesn't remember the drama that it inflicted. That could be a good thing, to not be burdened with memory. I wonder if some amnesiacs are happier people after they lose their memory. I suppose I couldn't very well ask them that, could I?

For the rest of us, when Richard first left it felt like we had a death in the family. It was so somber and surreal around here. I remember when my mom's little sister, our Aunt Alice, died at age thirty-five from breast cancer. It felt like the world came to an immediate, complete halt. Only, it didn't. The world just kept going in its regular way even after my aunt died. That very fact, the fact that the world could just keep on existing like that...well, that just seemed like a real asshole-y thing for the world to do. We loved our aunt to pieces. She'd tell us stories about how nutty Mom was as a kid. After she died, each morning when I got out of bed and made my way to the bathroom, the hallway felt like a dream hallway, surreal and strange. My body felt like it was trying to run under water. Everything was heavy. And witnessing my mom's sadness over the loss of her sister was even worse than experiencing my own sadness. I wanted to help her. I wanted to fix her. I still feel that way. But at least back then, Mom had Richard. He wasn't performing in a play that summer, so he was around to give all of us his undivided attention and love. He was extra playful and extra kind during that time. In fact, most of my memories, of him, pre-two years ago, were mostly good ones. I don't remember ever doubting my father's love for me, my sisters, or for Mom. But, just like my friend Carlie says, "All things are impermanent. It's not personal…it's just change."

Different than death, with abandonment, there's an added mystery attached to it. The people who are left behind are left with more questions than answers, and we have no idea how it'll all turn out in the end.

Carlie's words and the possibility of "impermanence" actually does help me keep hope alive. Maybe that's why people choose to believe in anything at all. It helps us keep hope alive.

My hope takes the shape of Maybes.

Maybe he'll come back.

Maybe he'll be sorry.

Maybe we can all be a family again.

Annie Wood

dream to remember

My mind plays the memory of that look in your
eyes when you disappeared.

An orchestra of gone,
                          gone,
                                    gone.
I listen to these pained cords on a loop.
Ringing in my ears, jogging my memory.
Remember when it was good?
What if it still is?
Only we forgot.
Let's make a deal to remember.
And then it,
and I,
and
we,
can be good again.

mom

This grocery store is the most crowded one in the valley and it perpetually smells of bleach, which makes we wonder if this market is really a front for something more sinister than fresh cabbage. Maybe that bleach is covering up the splattered blood of the crimes that take place after hours.

Or maybe they're just messy.

"Clean up on aisle three!" a guy says over the inter-com, right on cue.

Matty puts a box of Oreos into the cart.

"Nope. Wrong aisle," I hand them back to her.

"Come on. We hate the stupid health-food aisle!"

"Yeah!" Sara agrees.

"Don't just agree with Matty, Sara. Think for yourself."

"I am thinking for myself!"

"Okay. Then I guess you don't want any more of those animal cookies—the ones with the elephants."

"I love elephants!"

"Well, the elephants are only in the good aisle."

Sara turns to Matty and says, "Take me to the good aisle."

Off to the health-food aisle they go. Meanwhile, Mom is *whirling* around the store.

Mom took up whirling after we saw a documentary about a group of people in the Middle East who practice a religious dance by spinning around and around. They're called Whirling Dervishes. Ever since, when the mood strikes, Mom whirls like the wind.

"Join me, Matty. It's wonderful." she says as she whirls her way up the canned food aisle.

"It's okay. I'm good," I tell her.

"A whirl a day keeps the doctor away!" she says. "I'm pretty sure it's an 'apple' a day," I say.

"That's ridiculous. How could an apple do that?"

At least an apple is loaded with vitamins A, B, and C. What does a whirl have? Other than the ability to make the whirler dizzy and the watcher of the whirler utterly embarrassed.

She's whirling so fast now, she could possibly take off. Wouldn't that be cool? If she just lifted up and flew up high, right through the ceiling like the best scene from *Willy Wonka and the Chocolate Factory.* Only she's not inside of a flying elevator because she doesn't need a flying elevator. She'd be Willy Wonka in this scenario—all knowing with a magical secret. My mom is the music maker and the dreamer of the dreams.

"Look at me go!" she says.

Mom looks so happy. We used to have a bunch of fun times together, but now she's either locked in her room or having a good time in her own, little world. God, how I wish it were real. The happiness. How I wish it would last. I long to trust the whirl.

"Watch it, lady!" snaps an old woman with a cane. Mom whirled right into her as I was daydreaming.

I come running. "Mom, are you okay?"

"Her? What about me? I'm the one she bashed into," the lady gripes.

"Are you okay?" I ask the lady.

"Yeah, yeah." The old lady waves me off and begins to walk away. She shouts back, "You should put that one on a leash."

I want to kick her teeth in. But they're probably not even her teeth at this point and I'm sure she's used to them coming out of her mouth anyway, so the shock value wouldn't be so high. Plus, she's an old woman and I'm not the violent type. Also she's right. People can't just go around whirling into people. Still, that's my mom and, dammit, no one can say rude things about her. Except for me.

Sometimes.

And only in my head.

"Why don't you walk with me for a while? We can get some of those tangelos you like," I tell her.

Mom puts her hand on the cart and we slowly make our way to the fruit aisle. She's a little out of breath and sweaty, but otherwise she seems okay. Still, it's hard to know what the right thing to say is. It's like walking on a tightrope with her. At any moment, saying the wrong thing could trigger a bad reaction and then next thing you know, we trip and plummet to our bloody deaths.

She doesn't mean to be a bad mom. She wasn't always one. No, no, she's not bad. At least not on purpose. Can a person be bad if they don't know that they're being bad? If people don't fail us intentionally, do they still have to be held accountable somehow? She used to love spontaneous singing. She'd just break out into song in this very grocery store. Her favorite was "*Summer Lovin'*" from Grease.

Her: *Summer Loving, had me a blast.*

Then she'd point to me.

Me: *Summer Loving, happened so fast.*

Before puberty, this was the best thing ever and I couldn't wait for her to point to me. It didn't bother me when people stared at us because usually they were smiling. But after puberty, this routine embarrassed me to no end. I'd rather walk down the feminine hygiene aisle and ask for price checks on tampons from the cute cashier, Ashton, than be caught singing down the aisle with my mom.

"I'm thirsty," she says.

I hand her a bottled water from my bag.

She drinks then hands it back.

"Do you want to hold onto that?" I ask her.

She shakes her head no.

There was a time when I could talk to my mom about anything. She has a gift for non-judgment. I've never seen anything like it in anyone else. You could tell Mom your worst secret, your innermost negative discovery about yourself, and she would just listen, nod, and then softly offer a few soothing words. She could make just about anyone feel okay about themselves. Now our discussions consist of whether or not she's taking her medication, or if she's hungry or thirsty. We're down to the basics.

She has more issues than *Teen Vogue* but none of it is her fault. That's what they tell me, anyway. Something isn't working properly in her mind. She has a doctor, who seems legit. I mean, her degree isn't from the internet or anything like that.

Mom picks up a tomato and smells it. She grabs another. And another. Soon she has an impossibly large armful of tomatoes, some of which she's putting under her blouse, smelling them all first.

"Mom, what are you doing?"

"These smell delicious."

"Okay, we can buy some but don't put them in your shirt."

A bag boy walks by with a shocked look on his face. God, this is so embarrassing.

"You, uh…you know, you have to pay for those."

Yeah, we know that. Thanks," I tell him.

Matty reappears with Sara and adds, "We get how markets work."

"Yeah, we get how markets work," Sara echoes.

Feeling a bit outnumbered, the dude walks away. Matty turns to me. "What did she do now?"

"Nothing. Everything's fine. Why don't you get more of that cereal you like?"

Matty takes Sara off to the cereal aisle and I casually remove the tomatoes from under Mom's shirt, placing them back with the rest of their tomato family.

She begins pushing the cart again and I follow. "Hey, Mom?"

"Hmm?"

"Have you been taking your meds? All of them? The white, oval ones, too?"

She stops walking, turns, looks me straight in the eye, and replies, "They suck the joy right out of me."

"But, they actually make you...."

"More manageable?"

"Yes. I mean, I guess."

"They make me a shell of a person. Is that what you want? For me to be an obedient shell of a person?"

"No, of course not."

What am I supposed to say here? I'm not equipped for this sort of thing. I don't always know the right thing to say. In fact, I'm not sure that I ever do. So, I stop talking and we just keep pushing the cart down the aisle.

She's told me all of this before. The stuff about the pills turning her into a ghost of herself. She's told me she feels haunted by her own mind. But, when she doesn't take them, she whirls and hordes tomatoes and has the habit of going missing in the night. She's usually having some kind of fun, but not the good kind of fun. Like today. It's not the kind of fun that she seems totally aware of or in control of. It's not the kind of fun where she's a willing participant. She has a different fun. A manic fun that doesn't seem fun at all. But when she does take her meds, that's when we find her watching a blank TV screen. Maybe she sees something in the dark reflection of the flatscreen. At least she appears to be watching something, witnessing some story line unfold. Her face displays a variety of emotions; concern, puzzlement, sadness. Maybe it's shadows and memories that she's seeing. I sort of get it. Sometimes I get lost in shadows and memories too.

***

Matty and Sara come barreling back in with cereal and some extra stuff. I go through each of the items, one by one. After making a decision as to their worthiness for consumption, I take out my iPhone to do the math on my budget app.

"Tangelos!" Mom suddenly remembers and takes off for the fruit aisle.

The doctor says that she probably always had these synapses lying dormant in her brain, manifesting so subtly that it wasn't a concern. She says that some people who are prone to mental chemical imbalances aren't symptomatic until there's a trigger, a trauma of some kind. A big event in their life that sets them off. A big event in their life that pulls that trigger.

Bang. Bang.

Dick ruined everything.

dream to breathe

I'm lying in bed, restless, unable to sleep. Worrying/wondering about everything that's ever happened in my life and everything that will possibly happen in my life. Not that I can see into the future. Because I can't. I can barely see into my now. This is a recurring thing though, my inability to find quick slumber. When I check in on Matty and Sara, they're always sound asleep. It comes easy to some. I guess it takes a while for me to feel relaxed enough to let go. Being like this is a real drag. That's why I started watching YouTube meditation videos and writing down the things that Carlie's mom tells her. As a Buddhist, Carlie's mom has studied up on the whole "letting go" thing. But, the good news is, eventually, sleep finds me and then my favorite part of my day begins. I get to watch my dreams. My dreams, where poetry always rains down on me.

I'm only scared when I'm breathing.
I'm alive
and
that's
a good thing,
even when it isn't.
Maybe I'll like it more in the future.
Today…my daily actions are,
at war,
with my daily thoughts.
I avoid. I ignore. I accommodate.
In an attempt to remain even keel,
with my own wants.
with my own needs.
I fear that,
I won't get what I desire.
I fear that,
I will.
But it's okay,
Because,
I'm only scared when I'm breathing.

buried

{'berēd}
covered up or repressed

My toes curl around the faucet head as I finish up
the last line of my poem. Writing in the bathtub in the
middle of the night is a routine thing for me. All I need
is a blanket, a pillow, and my journal. The tub remains
empty because this isn't about cleanliness. The bathroom is the most private part of the house and there's a
lock on the door. These two facts alone make the
bathtub the most perfect working environment. The
writer Virginia Woolf said that to write, a woman must
have, *A Room of One's Own.* She wrote that essay in
1929 when the idea of a woman doing anything other
than making babies and "keeping house" was outra-
geous. The world has changed, thankfully, but in some
ways, it still holds up. If I were a seventeen-year-old
boy instead of a seventeen-year-old girl, I'd probably
be skateboarding with my buddies instead of playing
make-believe-mom to my sisters.

Anyway, I'm not a boy. I'm a girl who loves Virginia Woolf and who desperately wants to do what Woolf wrote about. She wrote that she wished to *bring buried things to light.* I'm not sure which buried things I'd bring to light exactly, but the idea of bringing anything to light feels...it feels like I'd be doing something of great importance. I like the sound of that. Of doing something of great importance. When I shared this wish with my English teacher, Ms. Brawell, she shook her head and said, "Sweetheart, you put way too much pressure on yourself. Forget importance, just make *something.*"

Ms. Brawell was the first person to encourage my writing. She noticed that all my folders were always covered in poems. Mostly e.e. cummings. He fills up a page in such a way that you have to actually look at it, not just read or listen to his words. He wrote in a connect-the-dot-kind-of-way, making artful word paintings that scatter across the page in all directions. He used lowercase letters like he was texting (only he died way before texting was even invented.). He liked to use parenthesis and play around with where he placed the words. Reading his writing is like experiencing an event on paper. It's beautiful.

I have a sneaky suspicion that this love of poetry was implanted in me through osmosis—all because of a crappy play that my parents did before I was born.

When I was little, my mom used to tell me the story about how she met my dad. They were doing an original play in a tiny theatre in the valley. The play was so bad that they didn't invite anyone they knew to see it. Backstage, after the show, the typical comment to Mom was, "Wow, you have so much energy." And to Dad, "Wow, how do you remember all of those lines?" Occasionally, a disoriented drunk would wander into the theatre to take a nap. The director was a real nightmare. He made boatloads of money directing TV commercials, but then he got busted by TMZ when they videotaped him raging-out on an actor while running lines at Starbucks. I don't know how someone could get so upset when in such close proximity to delicious chai lattés, but this guy did. After the Starbucks incident, the director bought a tiny theatre in Canoga Park so he could direct terrible plays that he wrote. But he actually paid the actors and the crew, so he still had people in town who were willing to work with him. Because...money.

My parents met at the audition for that director's first play and immediately bonded over their deep desire to book the job, and also over their deep hatred for that director. But they didn't fall in love until the moment my dad's character read a poem to my mom's character. That's what sealed the deal for the characters on stage—and that's what sealed the deal for the actors IRL. It was e.e. cummings poem, *i carry your heart.*

> i carry your heart with me (i carry it in
> my heart) i am never without it (anywhere
> i go you go, my dear; and whatever is done
> by only me is your doing, my darling)
> —e.e. cummings

I was born nine months later. One could say, poetry played a hand in the making of me.

Hoping to get in some more dream time, I climb out of the tub and make my way back up to my bed and crawl under the covers where I proceed to stare at the ceiling.

Breathe.
Inhale—calm.
Exhale—anxiety.

The first time I breathed intentionally was in a yoga class with Mom. At the end of the class, we all would lay on our backs to meditate. I remember feeling awkward lying there with a bunch of strangers. But, after a few moments, something cool happened while I was listening to the bells and chimes and the teacher's soothing voice. I felt like I could actually feel everyone around me breathing. I felt fully connected to these strangers. After watching my breath for a while, I began to notice something else inside me. I suddenly had so much space inside me, and I realized that I could fill up that space with whatever I want.

When I told my mom about it after class, she told me that I had an "enlightenment" experience. Google told me that enlightenment was another way of saying I had an "awareness" and experienced some sort of "wisdom." All of that from a little grownup nap time. Not bad.

Ever since that yoga class, I started researching meditation online and I found a YouTube channel where a girl my age named Harmony leads meditation for teens. I follow along with Harmony's videos when I'm feeling the need. Other than actively meditating, the only other times when I ever feel a sense of calm is when I'm writing. Or dreaming.

I feel my eyes getting heavier. Dreamland may be coming up soon.

Wouldn't it be so cool if someone could figure out a way to stay awake while we're dreaming? If I could,

I'd invite an audience with me to watch my dreams and I'd point at my dream and say, "Do you see *that* Lauren? That's the real Lauren."

I drift off to sleep and watch as Dream Me breezily types up poems on her old-fashioned typewriter from a top a willow tree. Because, why not, if you lived in a dream you might want to do most of your work from the top of a willow tree, too. When she completes her work, she pulls it out of the typewriter with a dramatic flair and gives it to the wind. Regular Me waits below the tree, utterly captivated by the floating paper. My eyes stay glued on the paper, which turns into slow motion snowfall, then it turns into a tornado of autumn leaves and then it's just paper again as it lands quietly on the grass at my feet. I always pick it up and then look up to make eye contact with Dream Me, which is super weird. Have you ever really looked yourself in the eyes? It's unnerving. I never know what to say to me. Sometimes I try to tell her something, but when I open my mouth, no words come out. Dream Me smiles down; I think she feels sorry for me. I spend as much time as possible in this dream state and allow the rain of stories to wash over me. It's like I'm witnessing my favorite character win at life. I can't help feeling envy for Dream Me, who gets to write whenever she wants. Wherever she wants. And live in a tree.

exquisite

[ik-skwiz-it, ek-skwi-zit]
of special beauty or charm, or rare and appealing
excellence, as a face, a flower, coloring, music, or
poetry.

It's morning again. This keeps happening—mornings.

I'm prepping Matty and Sara's cereal bowls, adding fresh strawberries. Strawberries are my favorite. The color, the sweetness, and the shape of them—they're such a cheerful fruit. I wonder what they're so damn happy about. They float on top of the cereal like they haven't a care in the world. Strawberries are exquisite. That's my word today: exquisite.

Words, words, words. I love them. Some more than others. Like, exquisiteness. Isn't that a great word? It sounds like what it is:

Exquisite: Of special beauty or charm.

I'd like to be exquisite and have an exquisite life.

"I need coffee," Matty says.

"Me too," Sara seconds.

"Neither of you need coffee."

"Why not?" Matty asks.

"Because, you're fourteen."

"So?"

"So, caffeine isn't good for kids."

"Who says?"

"I don't know…studies."

"Fine, bossy-butt." Matty yanks open the fridge and grabs some almond milk and drinks it from the carton like a wild animal. If wild animals had opposable thumbs. And refrigerators. And drank almond milk.

"Glass!" I remind her.

Sara lifts her hands up in the air as a signal for me to pick her up and give her a morning hug.

"Good morning, shmoops," I tell her, kissing her nose.

"Good morning, shmoops," she replies, kissing my nose.

Matty scoffs, sits herself down and eats her breakfast while tending to her social media addiction. I need to keep an eye on that chip forming on her shoulder to and make sure it doesn't one day turn into a boulder.

harmony

Hey, YouTubers! It's Harmony here with another mini vacay for your mind. So, sit up straight, relax your shoulders, take a deep breath in. Hold it for 1, 2, 3 seconds. Now exhale for the count of 1,2, 3. Good. Now, close your eyes and get ready to get your zen on.

Place one hand on your belly and one hand on your chest. Begin to feel the chest rise and fall. Begin to feel the belly rise and fall.

When we inhale, concentrate on the word "trust." On the exhale, concentrate on the word, "doubt."

Inhale-trust.

Exhale-doubt.

Continue with your natural breathing, feel the air enter through your nose, is it warm, cold? Does it tickle? Sit for a moment with the feeling of breath.

On the next inhale, feel your belly rise, then your ribs expand, and then your chest lift, coming to the top of the breath below the throat.

On the exhale, the breath leaves the chest, ribs fall, belly contracts. Now....

Inhale-acceptance.

Exhale-denial.

Continue with this breath, feeling all three parts of the breath, and think to yourself, belly, ribs, chest...chest, ribs belly.

Repeat this breath three more times. Now...

Inhale-love.

Exhale-fear.

Feel calmness in the breath. Feel ease and steadiness.

When you're ready...open your eyes.

You're calm, you're here, you're awake.

provisional

[pruh-vizh-uh-nl]

providing or serving for the time being only; exist-ing only until permanently or properly replaced; temporary.

Isn't it funny how you can love something at one time in your life and find it to be a major pain in the butt at another time? Summer is like that for me. During school, summer was everything. Now that there's no school and my sisters are home and need looking after, summer is exhausting. Who knows? Maybe in the future, summer will be something else entirely. How many things that we think we know for sure, are only temporary knowledge like placeholders, until we discover something new? I have no idea but I need to remember to write that question down in case I stumble upon the answer one day.

"I need a ride to Taylor's," Matty informs.

"Can't you walk?"

"Walk? You've been watching too many episodes of *Gilmore Girls*. This isn't a cute made-up town and nobody walks in L.A."

"Fine."

"I also need forty bucks."

"What? Why?"

"Movie, lunch...other such and such."

"What other such and such?"

"I know that Grandma Gayle gives us extra money in case something comes up so I just want my extra."

"Fine. Just finish your lunch."

"I want such and such too!" Sara says.

I glare at Matty. "Thanks a lot."

Matty's snark-fest won't last forever, but it's still tiresome. Sara won't be an echo chamber forever, either. They weren't this way before, so that's kind of telling that they won't be this way in the future, right?

Harmony says, "We never need to get caught up on how things are right now because they're only that way right now. And now is already over. Just like that. It's gone. Now is another now. See?" Then she laughs. I'm not sure if she laughs because what she said wasn't true, or if she laughs because it is.

Matty puts her dirty dish in the sink and then comes toward me with her hand opened. "Two twenties will be fine."

I'm so looking forward to that impermanence.

consternation

[kon-ster-ney-sh]
a sudden, alarming amazement or dread that re-
sults in utter confusion; dismay.

Annie Wood

the text!

hi sunflower
back in town. would like to take my
girls out for dinner
tomorrow night. 6pm antonio's?

They tell you to forgive
But they don't tell you how.
Maybe the only how
there ever is…
is
just
to
do

reconciliation

[rek-n-sil-ee-ey-shn]

an act of reconciling, as when former enemies agree to an amicable truce.

I read the text from Richard 46 times. Sitting in the tub early this morning while everyone slept, I thoroughly dissected it.

Okay, let's break it down:

#1. ***hey Sunflower.*** He calls me by the name he used to call me when I was a kid. I'm guessing it was intended to make me feel all of those old, happy feelings of closeness. Feelings of father-daughter love. But, it didn't. Nice try, though.

#2. ***Back in town***

Such casual phrasing. Like he was away on a short vacay. This is way too light and fluffy. *Back in town* is definitely a phrasing FAIL.

#3. ***would like to take my girls out for dinner tomorrow night.***

My girls? Does he mean me, Matty, and Sara, or does he mean Mom, too? After being gone for so long, he should really opt for as much clarity as possible. Also, he doesn't get to use the word "my" right now.

#4. *6pm, antonio's*

He didn't write, *How do you feel about this?* He also didn't write, *This must be a shock to you.* There was zero attempt to try to comfort or come back with any sort of ease. He was just straight to the point of what he wanted. Not even a customary, How are you? So in conclusion...

This Text Sucks.

Who does he think he is? It's not like part of me doesn't want to see him, but still, what about Mom? How could I do that to her? She needs me more than he does and I'm definitely on her side. She's the victim here. We all are. Everyone but him. Wait...so does that make him the villain? I don't want to cast any of us in these lousy roles, but at this point I don't know what parts fit. So, for now...I will just pretend that I never got that text.

***

I went about the rest of my day doing what needed to be done; braided Sara's hair, drove Matty to the mall, balanced the checkbook, made sure Mom did more than just watch TV all day.

Mom and I are taking a midday walk after I saw to it that she ate at least 3/4's of the avocado toast I'd made for her. The meds sometimes mess with her appetite. But, overall, she seems to be having a good day today, so I seize the moment.

"Mom?"

"Hmmm?"

"Do you miss Dad?"

"Hmmm...do I miss your father?"

She stops talking there. The pause goes on long enough for me to figure out that she's probably not planning to answer. Or maybe she forgot the question.

I try again, "I'm sure you think about him. I, it's just that we never really talk about him, so I was just wondering...do you?

"Do I...?"

"Do you miss Dad?"

"I think...maybe, yes. Yes, I do."

She stops to touch her favorite tree. Whenever we walk past this old maple tree, she likes to place the palm of her hands on the trunk. She tells me that she can feel the strength of the tree seep into her body.

"Do you still love him?" I ask.

"I do."

"How can you? After what he did?"

She smiles. "I'm gifted like that."

"I guess you are."

"I love him in a different way than before," she adds.

"Different how?"

"I love him the way I love a dream that I can barely remember. But what I do remember is how the dream made me feel. I remember that while I was dreaming…I was happy. So, I suppose, I love the memory, of the dream, of him. Do you understand?"

"I think so."

My phone vibrates in my pocket. Another text from Richard.

is no answer an answer?

He's using an emoji? What grown-up, adult man uses emojis? And the sad face emoji? If anyone should be sad face emoji-ing, it should be me!

I didn't notice Mom walk away from her tree, but she's standing over my shoulder now reading the texts.

"You must be curious," she says.

"I don't want to see him."

"Of course you do. He's your father."

"He can't just suddenly pop back into our lives like this."

"You rather he not come back?"

"No…I didn't say that. I just…don't know what to do."

She places the palms of her hands flat on my shoulders. "Here. You can have some of this. I got extra."

***

"It's not fair!" Matty yells.

"Life's not fair," Sara tells her.

"That's right, Sara. But it's not unfair, either."

"That makes no sense," Matty says.

She's probably right, but I don't want them to turn into negative adults just because circumstances sucked when they were kids. I'm trying to impart life lessons to them. You know, words of wisdom from their big sis. Even though their big sis is only seventeen and is just making it up as she goes along, like one big improvisation. But maybe that's what everyone's doing.

"If you all come with me, who's going to watch Mom?" I ask.

"She's having a good day. She's watching her shows. The TV is turned on and everything!" Matty exclaims.

"I think I should go first. I can go alone tonight and suss out the situation."

"We can suss together," Matty pleads.

"I want to suss! I want to suss!" Sara adds.

"He didn't text that he wanted to see only you, did he?" Matty asks.

"No, not exactly."

"What does that mean? Did he text: *You, Lauren, and only Lauren, meet me at Antonio's?*"

"No, he didn't."

"Did he say, *Bring Matty and Sara?*

"No names were mentioned."

Matty lunges for my iPhone.

"Hey!" I try to wrestle it back but she's a scrappy one.

She begins to scroll through my texts. "Aha! *Girls.* With an 's.' That's plural," Matty gloats, "Sara, get your coat."

***

Antonio's is an old family style Italian restaurant we all used to go to. They have big, red booths and the place smells of freshly baked bread and garlic. It has a loyal fan base of loud, happy regulars. Everyone is always boasting about how Antonio's makes "authentic Italian food." I'm guessing that's because the owner and head chef, Antonio, is an authentic Italian.

We're sitting in my mom's Honda Civic right out front of the restaurant.

"Why didn't he just come over? Did he forget where we lived?" Matty asks.

"Maybe he wasn't ready to see her."

"He could have called," Matty replies.

"I'm guessing he opted for texting instead of calling because maybe he didn't want our first words that we utter out loud to be on the phone. He wanted it to be live and in person. Anyway, he's here. We're here. It's time to do this thing."

"Let's go," I say. Then I proceed to not move an inch. I'm totally frozen.

"Are you okay?" Matty asks.

"Yeah, I'm just taking a sec to collect my thoughts."

What if this is a disaster? We don't know why he wants to see us. Maybe he just wants something from us, like to sign a legal document relinquishing his parental rights or something. Although I'm not sure that's actually a thing.

"Come on, I'm sick of waiting. You can collect your thoughts inside." Matty gets out of the car, opens the back door, and unbuckles Sara's seat belt.

"I want ice cream!" Sara announces.

I'm wondering if it was a mistake to let Matty and Sara come with me. I feel like I can't move. I remember an essay I wrote for health class on neuroscience once. In my research, I read that the rational part of our brains, the prefrontal cortex, isn't fully developed until age twenty-five. Before age twenty-five we are mostly dealing with our primitive brain, our reactionary survival brain. So, without the benefit of a fully developed prefrontal cortex, that means that right now, in this moment, I'm relying mostly on my primitive brain—the part that reacts to fear. It's the part of the brain that animals use to sense and respond to danger so they don't get eaten alive. They either fight for their life, flee for their life, or sometimes, I guess when it's all just too overwhelming, they freeze for their life. So, it's not my fault. I'm only freezing at this moment because my brain hasn't had a chance to fully develop. You can't rush nature.

Matty is holding Sara's hand and they're both waving frantically for me to get out of the car.

I can't let them go in there alone, so I take a deep breath and I knock three times on the dashboard for good luck, and get out of the car.

"He's late," Matt grumbles as we make our way to the empty booth. I look up at the clock and notice that it's three minutes after six. "Seriously?"

"Sure, it's three minutes, but it'll be more soon," Matty says. "He'll be even more late. You'll see."

"We're here. Let's try and make the best of it. And maybe you should let me do the talking at first."

"Fine by me. I have nothing to say to him. I'm just here for the breadsticks."

"Breadsticks. Yay!" Sara claps.

Sometimes I imagine us all grownup one day and wonder what our lives will be like. What kind of grownups are we going to morph into? With Matty, I mostly hope she doesn't hold on to this angry rebellious thing.

"Quit it!" Matty grabs a stack of sugar packets away from Sara.

Sara just looks at her, confused. "I was making a house."

"Don't be a jerk," I tell Matty.

"I'm not a jerk. People are going to want to use those and they don't want some little kid's germs all over them."

"I don't have germs."

"Yes, you do. Everyone has germs," Matty tells her. Sara turns to me. "Is that true?"

I hand her a napkin. "Can you make me something from this?"

"Of course I can." she happily accepts the napkin challenge.

We sit there, waiting in silence.

Two, four, six, eight, ten...diners tonight, not including us. One, two, three at our table.

There's a sole sunflower in a vase in the center of the table. Sunflowers. So upbeat. So hopeful.

There's a couple in their twenties sitting at a booth near us. They're holding hands and gazing into each other's eyes. They look like they're having an intense telepathic conversation. My sort-of-boyfriend last year, Danny Coleman, he and I didn't have that kind of connection. But Danny was an okay kid, in spite of not having telepathy with me. We never looked meaningfully into one another's eyes and our non-telephathic conversations were mediocre at best. One day after school, we were hanging out in Danny's room watching *The Big Bang Theory,* when he suddenly announced that he was a flower.

"You're a what?" I ask.

"I'm a flower," he repeated.

"Oh. Okay."

I guess he noticed the confused look on my face so he explained it to me.

"I saw a relationship coach talking on one of those shows my mom watches and he said that in relationships, one person is a flower, and the other is a gardener. The flower needs to be looked after, loved, cared for. The flower needs a lot of attention to bloom. The gardener is the caretaker. The gardener waters, feeds, and helps the flower grow. You're a gardener. I'm a flower."

"Oh. Okay," I repeated. But inside I was thinking, *wait, why does he get to be the flower? And who says he gets to decide this and just hand out the assignments like he's the boss?*

But I didn't say any of that out loud to Danny. And taking about it now, how completely un-fair is it that the gardener gets screwed like that? Gardeners need love, care, and attention too. Just because a person has the *ability* to be a gardener doesn't mean that they *should have to be one.*

Later that week, Danny and I had our first kiss. That's when the idea occurred to me that we should just go ahead and take care of the whole enchilada. We may as well check off all of the "firsts" together.

All my friends were always talking about how important the first time was. So, I was really expecting the earth to move or at least a pleasant queasiness in my belly or something. But no such luck. Our first kiss simply felt like two lips meeting and two tongues fencing. And the other first, the main one, well that was just a lot of bumping and giggling. (Danny, not me.) Maybe "firsts" aren't always "bests." Hopefully my best is yet to come.

It's now 6:25 p.m.

Matty catches me looking at the clock.

"Told you so," Matty says.

"Don't say that."

"Why not?"

"Boasting is beneath you."

"How do you know what's beneath me, bossy-butt?"

It's so weird to think that one day in the future, our three-year age difference will be invisible in its meaning. My mom's friends, Judy and Kristine, are sisters who are three years apart and you can't even tell. Because they're adults. But right now, this three-year gap may as well be fifty years. Matty still doesn't get that her "acting out" façade is obvious. Hopefully this is just a phase. Like me and my love of boy bands. I'm totally over that (except for you, Harry Styles. Call me.) Right now, being buddies with my sister isn't a priority. Right now, I just need her to listen to me so we can get things done. Like tonight.

"How long are we supposed to wait?" Matty asks. "Maybe something happened."

"Yeah, what happened is—he's a flake."

"I'm sure he wants to apologize."

"He owes us more than that."

"We agree that we want an apology, right?"

Matty nods and reaches for a napkin to turn into an origami swan. She origamis when she's anxious.

"Good. So, we'll wait twenty-three more minutes, and then if he doesn't show, we'll leave a note. That's the plan. We have a plan." I organize the silverware settings on the table so they're just right.

"Do you always have to be such a control freak?"

"Without control there'd be chaos. Do you want chaos?"

She's about to say something, but we both get distracted by the sound of the front door opening. It's Angelo's incredibly hot twenty-year-old nephew, Enzo.

"Wrong Dick." Matty laughs. "It's just your boyfriend."

"Shut up. He's not my boyfriend and you know it."

"Yeah, but you wish he was."

She's not wrong. Enzo is the most beautiful boy I've ever seen; he's tall, and tan with wavy, shoulder-length, black hair and big, caramel-brown eyes. We're not exactly friends or anything, but I've seen him around for years. Truth is, I've been crushing hard on him since I was twelve and he was fifteen. But I know I'm nothing more than a silly, little child to him. Like a kid sister. He never looks at me with any romantic interest whatsoever. The most we've ever said to each other is, *hey*. But man, oh man, I live for those *heys*.

Angelo appears from the kitchen and immediately starts yelling at Enzo in Italian, "Enzo. Dove sei stato?"

"Sorry, Zio."

"Sorry, Zio, sorry, Zio. You're always sorry, and you're always late. No more, capisci?" Angelo reprimands as he throws him an apron. "Entrare in cucina!"

On his ways to the kitchen, Enzo glances back at me and smiles a smile to end all smiles. A flock of doves are released inside my chest. I turn away before lift off.

Thankfully, Maria, arrives at the table with the breadsticks.

"Breadsticks!" Sara exclaims.

"Only one. Eat it slowly."

"The anti-gluten Nazi has spoken," Matty says.

Maria laughs. "Are you sure I can't get you kids something while you wait?"

"We're good," I tell her.

She goes back to join Angelo in the kitchen. Maria's always extra nice to us. Maybe at first it was because she felt bad for us having two screwed up parents. But lately I've been putting some other memories together. She used to flirt with my dad on more than one occasion when she didn't think anyone was looking. There's no actual proof as to how far the flirting went, but I have my suspicions.

"Do you think Grandma Gayle is making him do this?" Matty asks.

"She told me that he emailed her and asked if he could text," I tell her.

"He needs permission from his mother to text his own children?"

"Maybe he just wanted her advice."

Matty shakes her head. "Something is wrong with that man."

"Well, he is sick," I remind her.

"Yeah, whatever."

"Does he have a cold?" Sara asks.

"Mom's the one who's sick," Matty says, "probably why he left in the first place."

"Who left?" Sara asks.

Sometimes it's easier to ignore Sara even though ignoring her makes me feel guilty.

I whisper to Matty, "Don't say that. You don't know. Besides, there are worse things than going away for a couple of years."

"Two years is half of Sara's life," Matty says.

"I'm four!" Sara proudly proclaims.

"I know how old you are," Matty tells her.

"It could have been worse, is all I'm saying. He could have been abusive, or a perv."

"What's a perv?" Sara asks.

I slide over more sugar packets to Sara hoping she will keep building her sugar towers and take shelter there from grown-up disasters.

I glance up at the door and I see him, looking more rested and fit than I remember. He *pushes* on the *pull* door and bangs his head, "Damnit. Son of bitch!" He curses. That's when Sara and Matty look up and all three of us watch him as he rips his coat cuff on the handle, curses again, then slaps on a big smile and makes a beeline towards us.

"Wow, look at all of you," Richard says. "Sara? Is that you? You're so big!"

"I'm four!"

"Wow. How about that?" Richard smiles even broader.

I'm studying his smile and it doesn't seem all together fake, just a little weary. I want to touch his heart to feel if it's beating speedily. Or to see if he has one.

"You ripped your coat," I say.

"Oh, no worries. I have other coats."

"And you banged your head," Matty snickers.

"Are you okay?" I ask.

"I'm fine, I'm fine." There's a spot of blood on his forehead.

"You're bleeding," Matty says.

Richard grabs a napkin and dips the edge in a glass of water. He places the napkin on his head.

There's a slow, under the ocean silence that's deafening until he speaks again, "You are all so...beautiful."

We don't say anything and he keeps staring at us. He looks like he's about to cry. Shit. I really hope he doesn't cry because then I'd have to make it all better and I don't want to. I really don't. Richard notices the sunflower in the vase. He picks it up and hands it to me.

"I used to call you my little Sunflower, remember?" "No, I don't remember that."

"Oh. Well, that was a long time ago."

"And whose fault is that?" Matty begins.

"Matty, let him talk."

"Fine. Talk."

He must have known that this wasn't going to be an easy breezy good time.

"Oh…well, okay, I'm sorry…for being late."

"Forty-five minutes," Matty says.

"My audition ran late and then I got on the wrong bus…"

"How can you not have a car?" Matty asks.

She's relentless. But sometimes it's a much needed break for me. I can pretend to be calm, cool, and collected while she grills him. I adjust the silverware again and put the sunflower back in its vase.

"How can you live in Los Angeles and not have a car?"

Richard shrugs, "It's better for the environment?"

Maria comes back with some more breadsticks. Sara immediately grabs one and I glare at her.

"Pweeese?"

"Fine. Just one more."

She happily nibbles on it like a baby squirrel, only cuter.

"Ciao, Maria, you look sensational," Richard winks.

I bite my lip as a detour to the eye rolling I feel coming on.

"Richard. You look well," Maria says. "Still acting?" Richard loves to talk about his "art."

"As a matter of fact, I just did a big commercial and I've been involved in a few indies. How about you?"

Maria shakes her head. "Too much rejection. I manage this place with Antonio now." She glances over at Antonio, who's yelling in Italian at Enzo again.

"How's that working out?" Richard asks.

"Antonio is reliable, responsible, loyal. He's a good man. *Man* being the key word." Maria locks eyes with Richard, making him squirm.

In this moment, I may not trust Maria, but I kind of like her.

"Good." Richard looks unsure as to what his next move should be. He tells her, "You look sensational."

"You said that already," Matty says.

"Right. So, I did. Okay, how about a club soda with lime and some calamari for the table?"

Maria leaves with the order and doesn't look back. Richard, on the other hand, has his eyes glued to her ass. He catches himself and shakes it off, turning back to us quickly he says, "They have the best calamari."

"What is cal-a-mary?" Sara asks.

"It's squid," Richard answers.

"I don't eat squid," Matty says.

"Have you tried it?" he asks.

"Is it an animal?" she asks.

"Yeah, I mean, not really…It's a bottom feeder, in the ocean."

Richard won't win with Matty, but he doesn't know this new Matty so he's going to give it a try. I lean back to watch the match.

GAME

"I don't eat animals."

"Since when?"

"Since forever ago."

SET

"Well, it's not really an animal. It's a…squid. Besides, you don't know about a thing until you try a thing."

"I've never tried fried monkey balls, but I'm pretty sure I wouldn't like that either."

"Who taught you how to talk like that?"

"Well, it couldn't have been you."

MATCH

Silence. Aw-kward.

There's a family two booths down having dinner. Two parents, three kids. The dad jokes around with one of the little girls, making her giggle. The mom wipes the chin of another kid. A nice, happy family, having a happy dinner, happily together. They seem normal. I wonder what it would feel like to be one of the normals.

"I'm sure you have a lot of questions," Richard says.

Due to this being the understatement of the year, none of us respond. After another long, awkward silence, Sara throws a breadstick at Richard, hitting him on the nose. She smiles.

Richard picks it up from his lap and hands back to her, also smiling he says, "You dropped this." Then he turns to Matty and me. "Did you guys get my letters?"

"Yes."

"Oh. I wasn't sure because I never heard back."

Cue more silence.

After a moment, he continues, "So, how's your mother?"

Matty and I both answer too quickly and in unison:

"Great," I say.

"Bipolar," Matty says.

I shoot my sister a warning look. My mom's condition is a touchy subject, and I'm not sure I'm ready to open up to dear old pops just yet. Or ever. I use this moment to take out my headphones from my bag and place them on Sara's head. She's overjoyed.

"*Yo Gabba Gabba?*" I ask her.

"Yes, please," she says. I plug the headphones into my iPad and open up the Nick Jr. app. Now I'm certain that Sara can remain delightedly unaware. Lucky her.

"It's okay, I know it got worse. Your grandma kept me up to date. I understand that it's been a struggle."

"Ya think?" Matty says.

I'm sure Richard remembers mom's adorable "quirks" but he wasn't there to see them get less adorable. The day after he left, Mom went out and bought a silver BMW that we couldn't afford. She said that we all "deserved it." The following day she rode home on a candy apple red Vespa. I didn't even know she knew how to drive one of those. When she came home, her cheeks were flushed and she smelled like gasoline. "I didn't know where the gas tank was," she said. She started wearing turbans at some point. She said they kept the hair off of her head when she rode. She never asked us about school or how we were. She seemed so...preoccupied. But she also seemed happy. No, not exactly happy, more like...energetic. This lasted for a few weeks. We call this time, "before the fall." Grandma drove the car back to the dealership, some guy named Julio came to pick up the Vespa, and then Mom stayed in her bedroom for a year and half.

Changing the subject, I tell Richard that he looks different. He looks better. He tells us that being clean can do that to a person. I must not have been paying attention because Sara had her headphones off.

"You took a shower?" Sara asks him.

I place the headphones back over her ears.

Richard proudly places his one year sobriety chip on the table for us to admire. I steady myself so I don't allow a glimmer of hope to touch me because one year clean seems pretty fresh. One year clean smells like soap and baby powder. He could slip as easily as a ninety-nine year-old doing the tango on ice.

"Congratulations," I tell him.

"You've been okay for a year and you still waited to see us?" Matty asks.

"Well, I've been sober, but not exactly okay. I wanted to make sure I could handle this."

"Oh, right," Matty says, "I forgot, this is about you."

"You don't understand, I had to avoid triggers."

"You thought seeing us would make you slip?"

Two, four, six…counting breadsticks now hoping this moment will pass soon.

"It's a complicated disease—"

"It's a weakness" Matty interrupts him, "People just need to call it a disease to make themselves feel better."

Looks like that one bad moment piggy-backed right onto the next bad moment.

"If it's a disease then you get to remain the victim and not take any responsibility for being a self-centered, self-indulgent asshole!"

"You've given this some thought."

"She's given everything some thought," I tell him. "Matty's 'gifted.'"

"Don't put 'gifted' in quotes," Matty snaps. "I can hear the quotes."

I'm mad at him too, still, I don't know, I guess I want to hear what he has to say more than I want to yell at him. Or at least just as much as I want to yell at him. Which of course I won't do, because that would cause a scene.

"You're young, Matty," Richard starts, "you have no life experience to speak of, you can't possibly under-stand..."

"*No life experience?*" I had to watch Lauren give up her entire life just so she could raise us and our crazy mother."

"Don't say crazy," I remind her.

She ignores me and keeps pressing on. "You completely ruined our lives! All three of us have life experience, it's just a crappy life experience. Lauren's too perfect to tell you the truth."

"I'm not perfect," I say.

"I know you're not. You're a bossy, people pleasing, OCD control freak," Matty says, "you just act like you're perfect."

"No, I don't..."

"Look," Richard interrupts, "I can see that me leaving was hard on everyone. I get that. It was hard on me too."

"No," Matty stops him, "you don't get to include yourself in this. We're the victims, not you. You had a choice. We didn't."

Richard looks down at his hands as if they held tiny cue cards with his next line on them. But his hands are empty. He then puts his face in his hand and...surprisingly...

He begins to sob.

I've seen him cry in that TV special on ABC and once in a play in the valley, but I've never seen him cry as himself before. I feel helpless. And so sad. I feel like his tears might infect me and then my composure will crumble and I can't have that.

*Two, four six...*I count the crumbs Sara has left from the breadsticks. Sara looks up from the iPad and watches Richard cry. She pats him on the shoulder. "Don't be sad."

People are looking at us and I can practically hear their collective hearts breaking in unison.

"Great," Matty laughs, "now he's got everyone feeling bad for him."

"Hey, maybe we can forget about the past for a second and talk about now," I say, sounding a little more upbeat than I intended.

"Master manipulators. That's what they all are," Matty says.

"No, I don't want you to think all men are this way," Richard pleads through his tears.

"Men? I don't care about men. I was talking about addicts."

Matty's glare burns a hole right through him. He takes a deep breath and then tells us all about his big idea. He nervously taps his perfectly manicured fingers on the wood table top. Has he been getting manicures all this time? The thought of him sitting in a nail salon somewhere having his nails done while I can barely find the time to brush my teeth really pisses me off.

"I know I made a mess of things, but I'm ready to make it up to you. All of you. I'd like to take you all to dinner here at Antonio's once a week, every Tuesday night at six, at this booth, it can be our thing. We can talk about anything and everything over dinner. We can...regroup."

After a pause that lasted just short of forever, I say, "Sounds good."

Matty didn't like that one bit. "Sounds good? Seriously?" She turns to Richard. "That's your big idea? To talk over dinner once a week and 'regroup?' Well, there's no group to regroup." Matty takes off for the bathroom.

"Matty!" Richard calls after her.

Luckily Sara is back enthralled with her iPad.

I get a text from Mom.

i'm at the grove. where is everybody?

I quickly gather my things to get up and leave. "Sorry, I gotta run."

"Wait," Richard says in a panic, "where are you going?"

"I just have to take care of something. I'll be right back."

He glances over at Sara who notices and smiles at him.

"Maybe Sara would like to go with you?"

The sheer fear on the man's face might have been enough for me to grab up my little sis so her own father wouldn't have to be alone with her.

But, it wasn't.

So, I didn't.

71

heroics

{hə'rōik}
extravagant or melodramatic language, behavior.

Mom's dressed in men's boxer shorts and a now see-thru through tank top, since she was just salvaged from the fountain at The Grove, once again. She's dripping wet, sitting on the edge of the fountain with a well-meaning stranger who's drying off her iPhone with the hem of his shirt.

I always keep her favorite happy face beach towel in my trunk, just for these special, spontaneous dip-in-the-fountain occasions.

I go to her with the towel held out like I'm a fisherman spreading open a net to catch a school of crab.

Mom grins excitedly. "Lauren, sweetie! You're here!" She skips toward me and dives into the towel.

I wrap it around her shivering body.

The stranger approaches, handing me Mom's iPhone. "I dried it off. Still works. Mighty fine technology there."

"Steve Jobs. He was such a talent," Mom says.

The stranger takes me aside. "Listen, I know that the folks around here frown upon swimming in the fountain. I tried to tell her..."

"I can hold my breath for two minutes, Lauren. A record," she boasts.

"That's great, Mom." The crowd is getting larger and they're not opposed to staring.

The stranger continues, "I told the security guard that she was my friend so they wouldn't call it in."

"That was nice of you," I say.

He continues, "And I don't mean to overstep or anything, but you might want to...I mean, she was practically naked and that's not safe for such a pretty woman."

"Thank you," I say as I guide my mom away from the well-meaning stranger, thinking to myself that being naked in public is probably not safe for any woman, regardless of his opinion of their attractiveness. Sometimes I wonder if people can hear themselves when they speak.

Mom lets me lead her toward the parking garage. She feels so frail with my strong arm around her shoulders. It's like I discovered an injured baby deer in the woods and I'm carrying her back to safety. Having my dad's athletic, strong build, I could probably pick my mom up and carry her home if I had to. But, I don't pick her up. I walk her the same way I always do, slowly, gently, my arm lightly directing her every move.

She stops suddenly and looks at the face on the towel.

"Turn that frown upside down."

"Mom, that's not a frown. That's a smile."

"Is it?" she asks, puzzled. "How can you tell?"

I motion toward her boxer shorts. "Are those Dad's?"

"We're married. They're mine, too."

She's got a point. Technically, they are still married. I wonder if she remembers that we were meeting with him tonight. I don't want to bring it up because I think it might upset her. But on the other, if I don't tell her, I'll feel like I'm lying. Lying by omission. That's a thing, right?

"Mom, remember what I told you about the fountain?"

She nods, "we're not in Rome, this is not the Trevi Fountain and I am not Anita Ekberg."

Mom and Dad used to watch the Italian movie, *La Dolce Vita,* every year on their anniversary. In happier times, they'd act out the scene when the beautiful actress Anita Ekberg steps in the Trevi Fountain. Anita is followed in by the sexy Marcello Mastroianni. I like the scene, too. It's romantic. I heard that some American tourists, usually after having a bit too much vino, try this bit in the actual Trevi Fountain. It's illegal, so I'm guessing it doesn't end up being as romantic as they had imagined. But Mom likes to do the whole thing on a local level by calling a Lyft to take her to The Grove. Which I guess is a lucky thing for me because I don't have a passport.

She stops walking and gently cups my face in her hands. "You're my perfect, little fixer. You make everything better."

I smile even though I don't feel like smiling. I pop open the trunk, where I always keep a clean pullover sweatshirt and yoga pants for her. I guide her into the front seat and bring her the clothes.

"Here. I don't want you to catch a cold."

She changes her clothes as I drive us out of there. "Mom, remember how I told you that I was taking the kids out for dinner tonight?"

"Yes."

"Well, do you remember who we were meeting with?"

"Yes, you went out to dinner. You went to Antonio's."

Her voice is distant. Her lips move, but it's like the sound is coming from somewhere far, far away. It's so strange when she gets like this because it's like she's here and she's not here at the same time, and I'm never quite sure if I'm getting through to her. It's an unsteady feeling, like trying to walk normally in a bouncy house.

"Remember the text you saw? From Dad?"

"Your father?"

"Yes. We saw Dad tonight."

She doesn't say anything for a few moments.

"Mom? Did you hear me? We saw Dad tonight."

After a few more moments, she finally lets out a big sigh. Then she asks, "Did he get fat?"

"No. He's not fat."

"Because his grandfather on his father's side got ginormous when he got to be your father's age."

"Well, he's not fat, and also...he's sober."

"Hmmm."

I don't know what to make of her Hmmm. Is it a good hmm, a bad hmm, an indifferent hmm?

I was about to ask her, when she adds, "Don't let him trick you."

"Trick me? I don't think he's trying to trick anyone."

Promise?"

"Yeah, okay, I promise."

She takes another deep breath. "He's mighty handsome though, isn't he?"

"I guess."

"He has your eyes."

"Shouldn't it be the other way around?"

She shrugs.

I ask her if she remembered to take the pills I put out for her, but instead of answering me, she tells me the story again of how she first met Dad. The play, the poem, and how handsome and kind he was. I don't interrupt her, but I think it's weird that someone can fall in love with someone for being so kind, and then that very same someone ends up ditching their family.

I can sense her staring at me. Studying me. "It's harder for some of us," she tells me softly.

"What is?"

"All of it."

"He shouldn't have left. You needed him."

"It's not his fault. Not entirely."

"How can you say that? What he did was terrible."

"Yes. But he's more than that. Hopefully, I'm more than—" she looks down at herself, "—this."

"You're perfectly fine, Mom."

"I'm not fine, Lauren."

"Yes, you are," I insist, "we all are."

"Oh, Lauren. What am I going to do with you? You know, you're a lot like him."

"No, I'm nothing like him."

"Okay, you're not." She stops talking and gazes out the window.

After a moment I say, "Fine. How? How am I like him?"

She turns her face towards mine and smiles.

She says, "Why don't you find out?"

expectation

[ek-spek-tey-shuh]
the act or the state of expecting:
an expectant mental attitude.

By the time I get back to the restaurant, it's past closing time, but Antonio and Maria had kept it open for us. Richard looks so relieved to see me, his face practically self-combusts with joy. I'm sure Sara sang the entire cast album of *Annie* to him, and I'm equally sure that Matty remained in the bathroom the entire time I was gone. If she has her phone with her, Matty could be alone in the middle of the Mojave Desert and be content, as long as there was strong Wi-Fi. Plus, Maria probably brought her enough Diet Coke and breadsticks to keep her satisfied.

"Look who's back!" Richard beams.

"Lauren!" Sara claps.

"I've been thinking," I begin.

"Yes?"

"Okay," I say.

"Okay?"

Matty arrives back at the table and asks, "What are we okaying?"

I gather up Sara and her things, and then look Richard in the eye. "You want to see us regularly?"

"Yes. I do. Very much."

"Hey, don't I get a say in this?" Matty asks.

"He's been sick and he's trying to get better," I tell her.

"He didn't have cancer! He made a choice to drink and disappear for two years!"

"Don't be sad, Matty," Sara says.

"I'm not sad, Sara. I'm mad."

Richard steps in. "Matty, I get that you're mad—"

"Oh. Do you? Do you get that?

I start for the door with Sara in my arms and Matty right behind me.

I look back at Richard. "We'll see you here next week."

"This is bullshit," Matty grumbles.

Richard's face wears the look of heartsick worry and I have to fight off the urge to run to him, hug him, and tell him that everything's going to be okay. Instead, I put Sara down and instruct her, "Sara, go say goodbye."

She runs to Richard and he joyfully sweeps her up into his arms.

"Goodbye," she tells him.

"Oh, goodbye, sweetheart." He hugs Sara tightly, then places her back down. She's about to run back to me, but she has a sudden thought and turns back to Richard. She tugs on his pant leg for him to come down to her level. He kneels down and she whispers in his ear, "*Who are you?*"

If I could see through Richard's skin, I'm certain I would have witnessed the collapse of everything inside of him, fall and wither into a giant heap of sorrow.

"I'm Daddy," he tells her, his voice shaking.

Sara crinkles up her nose in confusion and runs back to me.

Even Matty looks like she might take pity on the man in this one moment. She stares at him, but says nothing. We all watch him walk out the front door. After a moment, Maria comes by with the keys, ready to lock up for the night.

"He really does mean well," she tells me.

I want to tell her that it isn't enough to mean well. That people need to do well. But then I think how no one wants to hear life wisdom from a seventeen-year-old, so I just smile and say, "thanks."

Then I want to punch myself in the face for thanking her.

harmony

Hey YouTubers! It's Harmony here. Today I want to talk about fear. What is it? Why is it? What can we do about it?

I asked you to leave your Qs in the comments so I'm going to read and answer one now.

"Hey, Harmony. My name's Emma, I'm sixteen, and I still can't swim. I don't really want to learn. The water freaks me out. My dad is always telling me to just jump in and that he wouldn't let me drown, so what am I so afraid of? But, I just can't. Is it okay to have some fears?"

Hey, Emma. I totally get it. When I was ten, my best friend, Susie Reynolds, was super allergic to strawberries. We were at Bryan Carsen's birthday party when Susie had some cake, not realizing that there was strawberry filling inside. Her face blew up like Violet's did when she chewed the blueberry gum that Willy Wonka warned her not to chew, *Violet, you're turning violet, Violet!* Remember? Anyhow, Susie had to be rushed to the ER. That image of poor Susie's blowfish face must've been branded in my mind because a week later, my mom made a fruit salad and I took one look at the fresh strawberries on top and fa-reaked-out. I flat-out refused to eat it. My mom insisted that it was my favorite fruit, but I was worried that I might also be allergic to strawberries. Like maybe I caught Susie's food allergy or something. My mom said that she promises I'm not allergic, but even if I was that, she'd make sure to save me. So, after a few seconds of thinking it over, …I dove into a strawberry. It was delicious. Now, if for some reason I had reason to not trust my mom, maybe I wouldn't have taken that bite. If your dad is with you and your dad knows how to swim,…then the only thing stopping you from diving in is…trust. Trust that you will be okay. Trust that you can learn new things. Trust that your dad's got your back.

Is it okay to have some fears? Totally. We should fear playing with fire and breaking the law. Those things keeps us safe and free. But as far as the smaller, life fears preventing us from reaching our dreams or enjoying life…I guess I'd be most fearful of…fear. Fear stopping us from possible enjoyment. So, let's try this: Close your eyes. Take a deep breath in through your nose. Exhale out through your mouth with a big sigh. AHHHH.

Imagine yourself standing on the edge of a pool with your dad by your side. You're gazing into the blue water, feeling relaxed. Allow the slow ripples on the water's surface to sooth your anxiety. You can see a reflection of a tree on the water. The tree's branches gently sway in the breeze. Your breathing is steady now, in sync with the rippling water and the swaying branches. You look at your father and you can feel his encouragement and his strength. This reminds you of your own strength. You look back down at the water and you get the sense that it's safe. That you're safe. You tell yourself, 'I am calm. I am safe.' Take another breath in, then out. Then...Jump. Now you're in the water and you don't panic. You stay afloat. You look up and see your father—his eyes never left you. You kick your legs and paddle your arms and your head is above water.

You're safe. You're swimming. Now...open your eyes, Susie. You're calm. You're here.

You got this.

parental units

One day my parents will be dead. I know that's a
morbid thought, and it's not like I'm obsessing over
this fact, it's just how it is. If I'm alive when they die
and if I come out of the writing closet slash tub, I'm
sure that I'll be the one who has to give the eulogies.
You're the writer, you do it. That's what they'll all say.
And what will I write in their eulogy? Dad was great
until he split. Mom was great until her mind split.

No, probably not that.

For awhile I thought my parents were normal.
Sure, my mom was more flamboyant than other moms
and my dad was vainer than most dads, but they still
seemed fairly normal. When Mom was happy, she'd
hold my face in her hands and look at me with such
tenderness, smiling ear to ear. Getting a smile from
Mom was like getting a standing ovation. It felt like a
gift she was giving only to me. It was a confirmation
that I was doing something so very right.

The most un-normal thing about my parents was
that they were still together, while all my other friends'
parents were divorcing. I used to think I was lucky

because I got to live in one home with both parents. I guess I was lucky. While it lasted.

Mom gave up on her dream of being an actress when I was born. I was born in Hollywood, California, which I guess made my parent's think that I was born to be a star. Or at least, I was born to potentially have the desire to become a star. I think it's funny that they thought my birthplace was some sort of destiny, since they were the two who planned where I was going to be born. I'm pretty sure destiny had no say in the matter.

Still, I sensed disappointment when I refused to try out for school plays and I tanked every commercial audition my mom dragged me to when I was little. Acting just isn't my thing. It's their thing, but not mine. I never actually told them that with my words, I just hoped they'd figure it out on their own. Most parents wish the exact opposite for their kids. They wish that their kids wouldn't want to be a performer because the chances of making it are so slim, a life of heartbreak is a strong possibility. But not my folks. They think performing is the be-all-end-all to a happy life. I guess I can understand the appeal of getting to be a character. Spending time as someone other than me could be a nice change of pace, and sometimes I think if I did act, maybe I could act myself right into a character I like better. Still, I've never had the urge to have a bunch of unknown people watch me do anything. I don't need applause from a roomful of strangers. Although, a pat on the back from either parent would be nice. But not because I'm doing what they want me to do. I'd like a pat on the back just for being me.

When I was a kid, Dad was working steadily in commercials and voice-overs, and Mom was busy with me. Auditions didn't come as often for her, and even when they did, it wasn't always easy to find a babysitter. I imagine she got busier when my sisters came along, but I don't think this particular type of busy ever fulfilled her. My mom was not cut out to be a full-time mom.

Sometimes I'd catch her in the middle of washing dishes and she'd be staring out the kitchen window, holding onto a mug with the water still running. She'd have an expression on her face that looked like she was on the verge of remembering something important. Something that was so close, like on the tip of her mind, but just out of reach. Like when you try really hard to remember a passing thought, but the harder you try to remember it, the faster it slips away. When I was a kid, I figured she was just daydreaming, but now, now I remember it differently. I used to love watching her pour her morning coffee into her mug. She'd lift the pot up very high, causing a long stream of coffee to flow beautifully down into the mug. She called it her "caffeine waterfall." I thought she was happy. An unhappy person doesn't pour coffee like that, right? But since her diagnosis, I started to piece our past together with my older eyes, and I see that what had appeared to be happiness, was actually something else entirely. Because that type of happiness never made her happy.

Mom's been diagnosed as having bipolar hypomania, which is basically an elevated euphoric mood state that may, or may not, be accompanied by serious lows. Hypomania isn't as intense as full mania, which I guess makes it harder to diagnose in some people. I suppose someone could wear hypomania in a way that makes them appear—to the untrained eye—to simply be a super energized, creative, somewhat kooky, happy person. But when you look closer, the energy doesn't come from a want, but from a need.

The choices a person makes while manic wouldn't necessarily be the same choices that same person would make when they're feeling balanced. It's a risk-taking, forget-the-consequences, scary way to go about the world.

Ever since her diagnosis, Mom's been on a "cocktail" of mood stabilizers and anti-depressants. She can go days where all seems well. But other times, the dosage isn't working, and her doctor then mixes up the cocktail in a different way. I like to envision the doctor behind a bar counter, shaking up Mom's meds in one of those silver shaker thingies and then pouring out a colorful concoction into a fancy glass with a mini umbrella and a maraschino cherry on top. All of this to keep the highs not too high, and the lows not too low, and to keep a depressive episode at bay.

Looking back, there were clues. Before Richard's departure turned all of our lives topsy turvy, Mom went through a few "passing junctures." That's what Mom called it whenever any of us went through any kind of phase. Like when Matty was obsessed with *Dora the Explorer* or when I went nuts for dinosaurs. These were just "passing junctures" on our life path, according to Mom. I kept notes on a few of hers.

Mom's Passing Junctures

The Clean and Cook Juncture-three months

My dad was away shooting a horror movie the first time it happened. When I was about eleven or so, I came home from school one day and found Mom in the kitchen, covered in all purpose flour, cooking oil splattered everywhere, every single pot and pan piled high in a big heap on the kitchen island counter. Before this moment, we pretty much just ordered take-out, or Mom would throw together some spaghetti with red sauce from the jar. I wasn't even aware that we owned this many pots and pans. Mom was in the middle of it all, smiling wildly.

"Lauren, sweetie! I'm making dinner!"

Then she proceeded to mash something up in a bowl, which later turned out to be rosemary, garlic mashed potatoes and honestly, they weren't half bad. Her sudden love of making meals didn't go entirely unappreciated, but her developing mania was a bit unsettling.

"Don't talk to me, girls. I must get the exact amount of baking powder and baking soda into this batter or the cake will never rise. Do you understand me? NEVER RISE!"

To which I usually would respond with an "um, okay" and then go straight upstairs to the bathroom, into the tub, and try to make sense of it all by writing frantically in my journal.

Mom never cooked when Dad was home. Instead, as soon as he walked in the door, she'd busy herself with cleaning. Suddenly it was of the utmost importance to wash all of the sheets and then let them air dry in the backyard.

"It's how they do it in Europe," she'd tell us. Then she'd scrub the tiles in the kitchen and all the bathrooms. She'd scrub so vigorously, you'd think she was removing the evidence of blood stains after committing a double homicide.

She'd scrub and scrub and until beads of sweat would pile up on her forehead. One time I felt so bad for her, I offered to help.

"No. I don't need your help," was always her reply.

I gained eight pounds in those three months and our house sparkled like the top of the Chrysler building.

The Shop Till You Drop Juncture-two weeks

A few weeks after the Clean and Cook Juncture, Mom eased up on the food and bleach, and discovered the joys of using her Amex Gold card and the thrill of receiving packages in the mail. Hello, Amazon and eBay! Her frenzied online ordering started around the time Richard started working on a new play in Santa Monica. His mind was totally focused on his role playing a 1930s mob boss and he was super busy with rehearsals, which I always suspected Mom didn't like, but she never said anything about it. Instead, she'd invest her energy into other things. Things like...*things*. So, while Matty and I were in school, Mom enjoyed her new hobby of getting stuff. All sorts of stuff. Such as:

Thirty-five Smurf figurines from eBay. The blue, tiny elves were her favorite toy when she was a kid. She said that she loved them because the Smurf family was so sweet and simple. She said the Smurf family brought her happiness. Matty asked her, "Doesn't your real family bring you happiness?" But Mom didn't answer her because she was busy ordering a digital Smurfette clock she found on eBay. I thought it was harmless. A lot of people collect stuff. Maybe even weirder stuff than Smurfs. Although, that Papa Smurf always creeped me out. Matty once put Brainy Smurf into the microwave because she wanted to see blue melt. The smell was so toxic, I remember thinking, This is how we're all going to die. Death by Smurf. Anyway...

Other things Mom purchased:

~Socks that light up when you walk

~A phone in the shape of a cheeseburger

~A super-sized bag of heart-shaped, multi-colored marshmallows

~A purple xylophone

~A curly rainbow colored wig for a dog (we don't have a dog. And even if we did—a wig? Seriously?)

~An inflatable sheep lawn decoration that's as big as a compact car

She was so delighted when the delivery person arrive. She would chat them up a mile a minute. "Oh, goodie. A present. I can't imagine what it could be. How exciting!" I was never sure if she was just pretending to forget what she ordered, or if she liked the idea of getting gifts so much that she actually convinced herself that they were from someone else. Maybe she was longing for a secret admirer. Or maybe just attention. From anyone.

The Smiths Juncture-one year

The year Sara was born, I thought Mom would become too busy and wouldn't have time to live out any kind of passing juncture. But, she managed to squeeze one in there. Mom was always into music, so I had heard her blasting one of her favorite bands, *The Smiths*, on her iPhone before. She always liked to sing along. But during this juncture, she did more than just sing along; she prayed to the gospel of The Smiths. Sometimes she'd cry after a certain passage. She sang, *I never never want to go home, because, I haven't got one anymore.*

For that entire year, a day didn't go by when she didn't find a way to incorporate The Smiths' lyrics into our daily lives. The thing is, The Smiths can be seriously depressing. She sang, *if a double decker bus crashes into us, to die by your side...*

The last one I remember hearing, got me worried. She sang, *don't try to wake me in the morning, because I will be gone.*

This juncture finally segued to...

The Sacred Bedroom Juncture-now playing

It takes the dryer to stop spinning before you realize how God-awful loud it was. After Richard left, Mom took to her bed and it got real quiet. The house got so still, I could hardly breathe. I began to miss the clanking of the pots and pans and the endless Smiths' songs. At first, she told us that she had a cold, not to worry. Then it was a "bad flu," but still, we weren't to worry. Then she told us that she just needed rest. "My body is changing, girls. It's natural. I'm okay. Really, I am."

I sprang into action, making sure that Mom got the rest she needed and Matty made it to school and that Sara was looked after, and I'm sure I was supposed to to deal with my own anger toward Richard, too, but I didn't have time for my own sacred bedroom retreat. I've heard people talk about accidents and they always say, "It all happened so fast." That's how my life drastically changed—so fast. A turbo charged shift took place the moment he left, and I couldn't slow down to see how it affected me because I needed to keep us all moving forward. It became my new obsession.

As far as my own life goes…

The Write Stuff fellowship has been bookmarked on my computer for a while now. The poems and stories that I've written in my writing tub are carefully marked in a secret folder on my desktop. The application—all filled out. All I need to do is hit the submit button. I'm just one click away from freedom. One click away from my dreams becoming fulfilled. Or at least, from attempting to fulfill the dream because I'd still need to be accepted into the program. But, so far, I haven't been able to make that click. How could I leave? I'm not my father. I even stopped returning Carlie's texts. The reminder of her and my life before just reminds me that I'm missing out. It's better to pretend. I pretend I'm happy, just busy. That's what I told her at first. But now, I just ignore the texts all together.

Carlie's texts:

come over this wknd? 🌻

how r u? 💜

miss u. ☹

I could change my phone number but instead, I just patiently wait for Carlie to eventually give up on me.

another poem. (e.e. cummings inspired)

(i bury your memory in me (i bury it deeply)

i am always without a clue (everything i feel i
ignore, my father and whatever stings
it stings because of you, my father)
i hear
i hear no song (for you are my silencer)
i create no stories (for you occupy my mind)
and it's you I blame whenever the moon is
hidden and whenever the sun stops singing
here is the deepest lie everyone knows
(here is the hurt of the hurt and the sigh of
the sigh and the star of the star of a flower called
joy which grows faster than heart can wish or soul
can ignore) and this is the hope that keep me
from falling apart
(i burry your memory in me (i bury it deeply)

the interview

When I see an old photo of my parents pre "me," I can barely recognize either of them. But they were full-fledged people doing people-y things long before I existed. A couple of years ago I interviewed Richard. I told him it was for a class project, but it was really just my way to get to know him because I could feel him drifting away. Maybe I thought that if I could know him, I wouldn't lose him.

ME
When you were a teenager, what was the most important thing to you?
DAD
Drama class.
ME
Why do you like acting so much?
DAD
I guess because I get to feel like a kid. Like I'm playing and I don't have to hold anything back. I feel the most free when I'm acting.
ME
What do you love most about Mom?

DAD

Oh…well, I guess when I met your mother she was…fun, and, you know, she was also an actress.

ME

I know. You did a play together where you had to make out.

DAD

That's right. She was great. I mean, acting-wise, not kissing-wise. Although that also was pretty good…

ME

Moving on.

DAD

Okay.

ME

What else did you love about Mom?

DAD

She was beautiful. She was so smart. And she was funny.

ME

What about now?

DAD

Now?

ME

You keep saying, *was*. Was beautiful, was smart, was funny…

DAD

Well, we're talking about the past, it feels like the right word to use.

DAD

ME

But now I'm asking about now.

DAD

Now...I don't, Lauren. Things...people...change. There was a time, your mom and I, we were very close, we had the same dream.

ME

To act?

DAD

To live creative lives. To always create.

ME

But then you created me.

DAD

Happily. Yes.

ME

Do you still blame the poem?

DAD

The poem?

ME

I carry your heart with me...I carry it in my heart...

DAD

I am never without it anywhere...

ME

Anywhere I go, you go…

DAD

You know, no matter what happens, I love you and your sisters very, very much, right?

ME

But what about you and Mom?

DAD

That's grown-up problems. You don't need to worry about that.

ME

But I do.

DAD

You just worry about you, okay?

ME

I worry about me, too

DAD

Don't worry about anything. Just, how are the kids saying it these days…you just "do you." Okay?

ME

Okay. But please never use that expression again.

DAD

Deal.

ME

Maybe we can all have dinner together Friday night. Like we used to. As a family.

DAD

I'd like that.

That night, I fed Sara in the kitchen, Matty ate in front of her computer, and Mom was in her room. Dad was out. No one knew where. We all pretended not to notice.

Your mind is a room,
decorated with care.
Childhood posters tacked on the walls.
Canopy bed now rusted and ruined
from the rain that let in
when you weren't paying attention.
"Clean your room!" I demand.
But you don't listen.
You can't.
or you won't.
I don't know.
But the room is too sloppy to ignore.
Important papers lost under piles of dirty clothes.
Music blares from your antique record player.
It hurts your ears but you turn it up louder.
"It drowns out the rest of the mess," you tell me
and you dance,
and you dance,
and you dance,
and you keep dancing,
as
fast
as you can.

indifference

[inˈdif(ə)rəns]
lack of interest or concern.

The night of our second meet-up arrives and Matty, Sara, and I are about to open the front door to Antonio's, but before we can, Enzo, looking as hot as ever, intercepts.

"Hey," he says.

"Hey," I say.

"What's up?" He smiles.

"Not much," I smile.

"Oh so eloquent," Matty says, scooping up Sara and pushing past us to the booth where Richard's already waiting.

"So…" Enzo starts. "My buddy's band is playing Friday night at The Whisky, you want to go?"

"With you?" *Duh, Lauren.* Geez. I'm so out of practice when it comes to talking to anyone other than my family. Especially a boy. Especially a cute boy. Not to mention, this is the longest conversation I've ever had with Enzo.

"Yeah, that was kind of the idea," he laughs.

"Oh, well...I don't have a fake ID, so..."

"It's eighteen and over."

"I'm seventeen. Almost eighteen though."

"Oh, right, I forgot. You seem so...mature." He looks me up and down. I always imagined that having Enzo look at me like this would feel great, but instead I actually feel weirdly exposed.

"Maybe we can do something else," I suggest.

"Yeah. Maybe." He looks inside the restaurant and notices his uncle making animated Italian gestures at him. "I better go. Later."

I make my way back to the booth.

"You and Enzo, huh?" Richard smiles.

"Yeah, you and Enzo," Matty mocks.

"We were just talking. Anyway, let's eat. I'm starving."

"Great," Richard says. "You girls order whatever you'd like.

I figure we can start with appetizers for the table." "Ice cream!" Sara yells.

"Ice cream is not an appetizer," I tell her.

"That's okay," Richard says, "we can mix up the rules a little, right?"

"Uh oh," Matty says.

"No, actually, we can't mix up the rules. Sara can't eat milk and sugar for dinner. She needs real food," I tell him.

"Milk and sugar are actual foods," Richard says.

I take a breath and turn to Sara. "You can have a small ice cream after dinner, okay?"

"Okay." She goes back to building her sugar tower.

"We'll have salads and whole wheat spaghetti," I announce.

"Bossy-pants is in the house," Matty says.

"Well, now that the food order is settled, ...I just want to say that I'm really happy you girls have decided to give me a second chance."

"*We* didn't," Matty says.

"In any case...I'm glad you're all here."

I hadn't noticed before, but he's balding a little up top.

I wonder if he noticed that. What am I thinking, of course he noticed, the man spends more time in front of the mirror than all us girls combined. This balding reality has to be making him crazy. I secretly hope Matty brings it up.

Maria arrives, breaking the silence. "Ready to order?"

Richard answers, "Spaghetti integrali e un'insalata per tutti, per favore."

"Oh man," Matty says.

"Italiano?" Maria says. "Impressive."

"I did a romantic comedy in Italia this past summer," Richard boasts.

Maria doesn't ask for any details. She takes the food order and quickly heads back to the kitchen.

"Are you sleeping with her?" Matty asks Richard.

"Matty!" I say.

"It's okay. No, Matty, I'm not sleeping with anyone."

"But you did," she says.

"I did a lot of stupid things for a lot of stupid reasons when I was drunk."

"That's an excuse," she says.

"I don't mean it to be."

Before Matty and Richard get a chance to hop onto the blame game ride, a group of loud frat boys storm into Antonio's.

"Hey! A pitcher of beer for my friends!" demands one of them.

"Just a sec!" Maria calls back to them.

"I'll give you all the time you need, sweetheart. I'll give you a real good time, if you know what I mean." He and his buddies laugh.

"Are you a cougar?" asks another one.

"Because cougars love to eat us up!"

They all laugh obnoxiously and punch each other in the arms. Not hard enough for my liking. I'll bet they started drinking hours ago at Jack's Bar and Grille across the street, but then finally got kicked out for their obvious lack of people skills.

"Hurry up, woman!" yells one drunken idiot.

"Serve us like God intended!" yells another moron.

"Gross," Matty says.

"I agree." Richard gets up. "Excuse me, girls." He makes his way toward the guys. I'm 65% worried and 35% proud. Although, Richard is a middle-aged actor and these guys are young and buff and mean. Okay, maybe 75% worried.

"Hey guys. What do you say you keep your voices down and show a little respect?"

"Right, Gramps. Whatever you say."

"Gramps? I'll have you know that my age range is thirty-five to forty-five, so that makes no sense whatsoever."

"He did *not* just give that guy his age range," I say. Matty tries to stifle a laugh but fails.

"My old man is forty-five," says one of them.

"Well, I didn't say that I was forty-five. That's the last number in my age range. Clearly you don't understand how age ranges work."

"Get out of our faces, old man."

"I will, gladly, if you promise to keep it down and show some respect."

One of the jerks gets off of his bar stool and is about a foot taller than Richard and two feet wider—a total jock who looks like he could flatten Richard with an aggressive thought.

My heart starts beating quickly. All of the bozos are now gathering around Richard, displaying their chests, all puffed up and pumped up like gorillas preparing to pounce.

Richard might be doing all of this to impress us, and I have to admit, it's kinda working, but I don't want to have to witness his death right now. I feel that might be a tad traumatizing. I think about saying something, but before I have a chance to think it through, I notice my dad staring at the big guy's neck tattoo. It's of a cross and Jesus's face. I can practically hear the wheels turning inside of Richard's mind. He's concocting something.

"Okay, you're right. My mistake. The beer's on me," Richard says.

"That's more like it!" They all go back to their bar stools and wait for their free beer to arrive.

Maria brings over the pitcher. Richard swiftly takes it from her and says, "Actually, I changed my mind, the beer's on you." He then pours the pitcher of beer all over the biggest, meanest one!

One of them throws a punch at Richard's face, but Richard ducks masterfully and the guy's fist hits the bar instead.

"OWWW!"

"Dude? Why'd you hit the bar?" his friend asks.

"I didn't do it on purpose, you idiot!"

Antonio comes running out, "Basta! Or I call the polizia!"

Two of the guys back off, but the one with the Jesus tat is too jacked up on booze and testosterone to hear him.

He moves toward Richard and I'm certain that our desserts will have to be delivered to the ER.

Suddenly, Richard starts spastically jerking his body around like he's having some sort of seizure. "The devil's got me again!"

I notice him give a quick glance over at Maria, who immediately jumps in, "Oh, no! Not again!"

"Wha's happening?" the big guy says.

Maria glances at Antonio who adds, "It's the curse! Don't touch him or you'll get it, too!" Antonio and Maria step back, frightened expressions on their faces.

The beer-soaked guy looks legit scared now. He backs away from Richard, who is now on the ground spazzing out and blurting nonsense that I think is supposed to sound like Latin. He's using his "devil voice." It used to freak us out so much that he would only use it once a year, on Halloween, and only during daylight.

"This place is wacked!" Yells one of them.

They all high-tail it out of there, getting as far away from the possessed old man as they can.

As soon as the guys are gone, we all bust out laughing. "That was epic!" Matty exclaims.

"Uomo pazzo. But…you are clever," Antonio says. Maria throws Richard a towel. "Clean up your mess."

"How did you know he'd go for it?" I ask.

"Me and his dad used to shoot hoops. I remember when he told me about his son getting that tattoo to help him 'ward off the devil.' Apparently that boy has a deep-seated fear, so I figured he'd probably want to steer clear of anyone who could possibly be Satan adjacent."

"How'd you avoid the punch?"

"Learned a few moves in a Kung Fu web series I was in. I'll send you the link."

You know, there's a strong possibility I might actually watch it.

Piles of clothes, lie lakeside.
Swimming nude
without
embarrassment
because
I am awake,
not shy.
What's the point of shy?
Nothing matters.
(but everything's important)
Naked in the water and
the sun shines through me,
a penetrating spotlight,
branding me with the words,
soon is my time,
soon is my time,
soon is my time.

encore

['änkôr]
any repeated or additional performance or appearance.

"I understand that your mother has been struggling with various issues, and I'm trying to be patient, but I can't have a woman parading around in undergarments, splashing about in a public fountain," The Grove security cop tells me on the phone.

"I understand. I'm so sorry. I'm on my way now."

Matty agrees to stay home and watch Sara as long as I buy her those jeans she wants. So she didn't so much as agree as bargain. Sometimes that's what life feels like to me—a series of bargains. I make bargains with myself all the time. If I finish the dishes by eight o'clock, I can take a ten-minute shower. If I read Sara three bedtime stories, I can eat the last cupcake. I have no trouble keeping these tiny promises. It's the bigger promises to myself that I'm too afraid to ever make for fear of letting myself down.

I arrive at The Grove near closing time, so thankfully there's not too many people around.

I make my way over and Mom's smiling like she just won Powerball.

"Hi, Mom. Let's get you dry."

"Lauren!" She bypasses the towel and gives me a forceful, wet hug. It's too wet and too excessive but I let her do it anyway. Finally, I gently push her back and wrap the towel around her. The security cop is giving me the evil eye.

"Can we have a little chat?" he asks.

"Sorry about my mom. It won't happen again."

"You said that the last time."

"She just gets a little confused sometimes."

"There's a public swimming pool at the Encino Park. Maybe she can get confused there."

"Good suggestion. I'll tell her."

He adds, "I don't want to have to call the police."

"Thank you for not doing that."

"I have a cousin who's a little loopy. They have all sorts of medication these days…"

"Really? Thanks for letting me know. I'll look into it."

He nods and tips his hat like a gentleman cowboy from the old west. I give him a quick curtsy and escort Mom to the parking garage.

We drive home in silence for a while. She's gazing out the window the way I remember doing as a kid— eyes wide with expectation, soothed by the rush of passing things, and carried lightly by the rhythm of the car. Nothing to do and nowhere to be. Just a kid in a car, going wherever the grownups are taking you. Times like these, I feel like my mom isn't my mom at all. She's my little girl and it's my job to take her where she needs to go.

"Mom?"

"Hmmm?"

"Maybe we should look into a new therapist."

"Such busybodies. Always asking questions. Always wanting to know every little thing about me."

"That's their job."

"Lauren, I just wanted to go for a dip. Haven't you ever just wanted to walk in the Trevi Fountain?"

"That's not the Trevi Fountain, Mom. That's in Rome. We're in Los Angeles. In America."

She thinks hard for a moment, her forehead wrinkles as she remembers.

"Of course. I know that." I can hear the disappointment in her voice.

I don't blame her. I guess if I just thought I was doing something exotic somewhere amazing I'd also be disappointed if someone reminded me that I was just in my regular ole life. Except, this regular ole life used to be enough for her.

Enough.

When I had sleepovers at Carlie's, her mom used to toast our orange juice in the morning with, "May you always have enough."

I didn't really get it back then. I remember thinking, *Enough of what?* But I guess the toast is trying to say...may we be satisfied. I'm not sure I ever met anyone who seemed to be satisfied. People are always going around looking for something different. Something more.

"We can try another medicine cocktail. I think we haven't gotten the mix quite right. It's not your fault," I tell her.

"Cocktail," she laughs, "you make it sound celebratory. It's not celebratory and I don't indulge in non-celebratory cocktails."

I pull the car to the side of the road and shut off the ignition. "Are you saying that you haven't been taking your medicine?"

She grabs my hands. Hard. "Do you feel that?"

"Yes. Of course I feel it. You're squeezing my hands."

"What do you feel?"

"I told you. Your hands squeezing my hands."

"Yes. What you're feeling there, that's my strength. I want you to feel it." She grips even harder.

"I feel it. I feel it!" I tell her as I pull my hands free from her death grip.

This was a more aggressive display than I'm used to. She's usually more like a butterfly than a bull. Seeing her in this new light rattles me.

Two, four, six...sets of headlights passing by.

"I know you're strong, Mom. That's not the point. This isn't about physical strength...it's about your mind."

She turns on the radio and is overjoyed by the song that's playing.

"I knew it!" she screams giddily. "I knew that if I turned the radio on at this very moment, I'd get a sign from the Universe!"

Mom sings passionately along with Bon Jovi, *It's my life and it's now or never but I ain't gonna live forever, I just want to live while I'm alive...*

"Mom, we really need to talk about this." I reach my hand out to shut the radio off, but she swats it away like a mosquito.

There's no talking to her when she gets like this. If I learned anything from The Smiths juncture, it's not to get in the way when she's expressing herself through song lyrics. Besides, Bon Jovi may have a point here. It is her life.

I'm surrounded by a thousand pillows.
I'm embraced by muffled cries of queasy doubt,
Held up,
high,
on a steely pedestal.
Sharp And Jagged.
I steady myself with the will of a thousand
acres of have-tos
and shoulds
and choicelessness,
I can see everything from way up here.
Everything, you all need.
Everything, you all want.
Far, far away I can hear a tiny voice from the invis-
ible distance deep inside of me.
That voice pleads to me now;
Please,
see *me,*
Please,
hear *me.*
I am here too.
when will you make room for me?

harmony

Hey YouTubers! It's Harmony here. Today I want to talk about...appreciation. Grownups are always telling us to "appreciate what we have." For me, I usually hear this line right after I ask my mom for a new pair of boots. But I think appreciation goes way beyond being grateful for the material things. I started thinking...do I appreciate the people in my life for just...being in my life? Also, do I, myself, feel appreciated? Sometimes I feel like I try to show up for my friends in all the ways they need me to, but I don't get that in return. That makes me feel horrible. So, what do I do? I thought about confronting them, but what would I say? "Why didn't you thank me for helping you with Chemistry homework yesterday?" That felt petty, so instead I hatched a new idea. I thought, since I'm a believer in putting out what you want to get back, ...I decided to be more appreciative of them.

I made these Awesomeness Cards that I carry around with me and whenever I notice someone doing something I feel like acknowledging, I leave one somewhere where they'll find it. It's not important that they know it came from me, —it's just important that they know that someone noticed.

You can help keep the #AppreciationTrain going!Make copies, pass it on. If they catch you in the act, some people might think you're weird, but, so what? All the best people are.

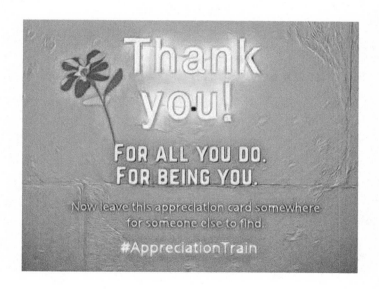

She wishes she named herself
then she could be beautiful
the way a *Gloria*
is
beautiful.
a lyrical name may have lead
to a lyrical life,
instead of this one, which…
so far,
offered a steady stream of disappointment and regret.
Still, the optimist waits
(with great hope)
for her
lyrical
life to begin.

discommode

{diskə'mōd}

to cause inconvenience to; disturb, trouble, or bother.

"Can we get the rainbow bubbles?" Sara loves it when I take her to the drive-thru car wash. She squeals with delight when the red-blue-green soap suds fall down onto the windshield like Rainbow Dash melting over glass.

I had to get out of the house. I spent the good part of this morning trying to persuade Mom to take her pills. It was mostly me reasoning on a loop, while she sat there watching me as if my forehead was projecting her favorite movie. I was putting on a one-woman show in her bedroom, and she was the polite, attentive audience member who didn't dare interrupt the performance.

The rest of the morning was spent arguing with Matty over seeing Dad for our weekly dinner scheduled for tonight.

"This will be our third one and he still hasn't apologized. I'm not going," Matty says.

"What if tonight's the night?" I say.

"It won't be," she says as she storms off to her room, which for some reason makes Sara burst crying.

So, in an effort to distract, here we are, enveloped in a kaleidoscope of multicolored foam.

"We should come here every day," Sara says.

"I think we need to give the car time to get dirty."

"Why? You take a shower every day."

"That's true."

"Are you dirtier than Mommy's car?"

"I guess I am."

I get out of the now shiny car and proceed to tidy up the insides by vacuuming. I'm bent down, fishing for junk between the seats when I'm startled by a guy's voice. "Hey, Lauren."

I jump and bang my head on the steering wheel. "OWW."

"Wow, sorry. You okay?" Enzo asks.

"Oh...me? Sure. Of course. Why wouldn't I be?"

"Um...because you banged your head."

"No, I didn't."

"Yes, you did!" Sara confirms from the passenger seat. "Hi, Enzo," Sara waves.

"Hey, Sara. What's up?"

"We had rainbows!" she tells him.

I stand up, head tingling, hands full of sticky gum wrappers and used Kleenex. "We were just...washing the car."

"I see that," Enzo says all cool-like. Ugh, he's always so chill. It's unnerving.

He removes some random debris off my shoulder. "Oh. Thanks."

"Anyhow, my friend, Carla, is having a party this weekend in Santa Monica."

He stops talking here and I'm wondering if I'm supposed to say something.

"Cool."

"So, you in?" he asks.

I'm pretty sure he's asking me out on a date right now and I'm pretty sure there's no way I can go. What if Mom wanders off while I'm away? Matty would probably find the hidden emergency cash and buy the new iPhone, and she'd feed Sara a box of sugar cubes for dinner.

"Sorry. I have—"

"—Family stuff. Yeah, yeah. I figured you'd say that.

You're like some kind of saint or something." Enzo starts to walk away.

I call after him, "I'm not a saint!"

125

I want my words to stop him dead in his tracks. I want them to make him turn around. I want them to inspire him to come running back and ask me out again. But they don't. Enzo continues to walk away, glancing back for only a moment he says, "Whatevs. Later, Saint Lauren."

***

Antonio's is busy tonight, but Maria made sure to put a reserved card on our table so we can sit in our regular booth. I think I'd like Maria, if not for the fact that she's a home wrecker. No, that's not fair. She's not even the woman he left us for. He left for some actress he was doing in some play he was doing. I guess, if I really think about it, Maria was also left. Of course, it's not the same as leaving your wife and kids. Still, she's really nice to us. Is it possible to sort of resent a person that you sort of like?

I'm still picking at my salad, arranging the shaved carrots into little mounds on my plate. Sara's lost in bliss over her ice cream, and Matty's texting her girlfriend. Actually, boyfriend. Matty's best friend, Taylor, was born a girl, but is transitioning into a boy. Or I guess more accurately, he's in the process of physically becoming what he always was. Anyhow, I'm pretty sure that they're more than friends now, which means Matty's currently going through all the stages of young love and possibly wondering where she fits in. She hasn't asked for my thoughts on any of this yet, and I'm kind of glad. I don't know how she should navigate through this new territory because it's all new territory for me, too. Not just the transgender part but the dating part. The falling in love part. I want to be her mom slash big sis here, but I'm also afraid of putting my nose into her business. But maybe it belongs there. I don't know the rules. I hate it when I don't know the rules.

Richard looks like he's been thinking hard about what to say to us. After ions of the only sounds being my fork scraping the plate, Sara's "mmmm" over her ice cream, and Matty's thumbs tapping her iPhone, Richard finally speaks.

"So, Grandma tells me she found a great place for your mom. She said she sent you a link to the website?"

"Mom has a home. She's in it," I say.

"Yes, of course, Lauren, I know. I don't mean permanently. It's just, maybe, for a little while she could go to this place and get looked after. New surroundings, new doctors, might be good for her."

"We're good for her," I tell him. I turn to Matty. "Matty, no phones at the table."

"You're not my mom, bossy-butt," she says, not bothering to look up.

"Who are you texting, anyway?" Richard asks.

Matty looks up and smiles. She pushes her phone to the side and gives Richard her undivided attention. She leans in. I know this means she's prepping for something.

"I was texting my boyfriend."

"Oh? You have a boyfriend? That's great. What's he like?"

Sara joins in the fun. "Taylor used to be a girl!"

"What's that now?" Richard asks.

"Taylor was born a girl. Now, he's becoming on the outside who he really is on the inside," Matty tells him.

"Oh. I see. And...um...so...what about her parents? What do they say about that?"

"*His* parents are supportive. They want him to be happy."

"Did she...he...have the, you know...surgery?"

"That's a personal question, Richard. And it's not just about body parts," Matty says.

"Things sure have changed," Richard laughs uncomfortably.

"Well, you've been out of the loop," Matty says.

"Please stop calling me Richard. I'm your father." Matty guffaws.

I shoot her a dirty look and attempt to hijack the conversation by turning to Richard. "You mentioned you were in therapy?"

"Yes. Well, sort of."

"You're sort of in therapy?" I ask.

"Well, I'm in this play, it's an equity waiver house in NoHo, great show, brilliant writing. I hope you guys will come see it."

Total silence.

"Anyway...I started researching this role. I'm the lead, real challenging role, very gripping, and my character, Steven, is deep into therapy. So Steven's therapist strongly suggested that Steven do whatever it takes to clear up his past. So, as research, I started to see a therapist. And my therapist suggested that I do the same."

"So, you're here because your therapist suggested it?" I ask.

"No," Matty adds, "*Steven's* therapist suggested it. "Strongly suggested it," Richard adds.

"UN-FUCKING-BELIEVABLE!" Matty storms off toward the bathrooms.

"The bathroom again?" Richard asks, turning to me. "Is this a regular thing?"

"She's a runner," I tell him.

"Ah, like your mom."

"Right." I'd like to hold a mirror up to his face, but I don't have one handy. How can some people be so clueless?

***

"Matty, come out."

"No. I hate him!" she yells through the stall door, in tears.

"No, you don't."

"Yes, I do."

"Fine, you hate him. But only because you love him."

"He doesn't care about us!"

"Then why is he here?"

"Because of step nine."

"What are you talking about?"

"In AA, step nine is when addicts are supposed to make amends to everyone they've harmed. That's what he's doing. Only he's not doing it right."

"What do you mean?"

"You can't do it if it the amends is going to hurt someone. And he's hurting us."

"Maybe he's actually sorry, Matty."

"He didn't say so. And he didn't say so because he's not. He had fun without us holding him back."

"You don't know that."

"He's only here because a fictional therapist told his fictional self to be here," Matty says.

"Okay, but still a fictional or real therapist can't make you do things you don't want to do. Come out of the stall, Matty."

"I'm not done."

"Fine." I sit myself down on the bathroom tile.

"While I'm waiting for you to be done, why don't you tell me something I don't know?"

After a moment, in a calm voice, Matty says, "Did you know...that most people go to the bathroom twenty-five hundred times per year and spend at least three years of their lives on the toilet?"

"Wow. No. I didn't know that."

Matty slowly opens the stall door and stands there staring at me with her puffy eyes. I get up to meet her.

She hides her face behind her hands.

"It's okay, Matty. I've seen you cry like a million times."

"I'm not crying," she cries.

I put my arms around my little sis. "I know you're not."

We go back to the booth and we arrange with Richard to meet next week at our home. He wants to see Mom. Won't that be fun?

Yeah. I don't think so either.

I like the dusk best of all.

Each time it arrives, if I happen to be there to catch

it,

I feel like it

sneaks up on me

and

I'm instantly covered in a mysterious layer of the

day.

I surrender instantly, allowing it to embrace me

fully.

We slow dance, the dusk and I for thirteen minutes

and eight seconds,

forgetting all about the dawn,

the day and

the night.

Now is just for us.

Now is for this slight dimming of the lights,

this warm wind,

this quiet change.

I know this is only temporary,

as I know everything is only temporary.

It doesn't make me love it any less.

(Maybe it makes me love it more.)

This moody, not-quite-night-time

holds me closely in its light dewiness

and in its faraway smell of someone's

supper in the air.
I am all at once far, far away, wrapped up in a curious, distant cloud
and I am
close, close here, I am home.
Soon darkness will declare its victory over you and
that darkness will last much longer than thirteen
minutes and eight seconds.
It will go on, and on,
for several hours...
leaving dusk—in the dust.
And I will forget all about this time we shared as
my eyes adjust to the
night.
I will forget until the next time you sneak up on me
and I am reminded...
I like the dusk best of all.

reciprocity

*[res-uh-**pros**-i-tee]*
reciprocation; mutual exchange

It's the morning of our family dinner, and I woke up with a queasiness in my stomach. I can't remember the last time we were all together as a family, and I'm not sure it's something that you can just jump back into. Also, Richard hasn't seen Mom in two years. A lot has changed. What he used to chalk up to quirkiness has morphed into something far less cute.

Instead of asking Matty to help me with dinner, I agree to drop her off at Taylor's place with the deal that she won't act jerky at dinner. I drop Sara off at a playdate. I stopped leaving Sara alone with Mom after Mom wandered off to the grocery store one day because she had an immediate craving for ants on a log. She left to get peanut butter, celery, and raisins, and thought that Sara would be fine home alone. "I left the TV on for her," she told me in her defense. Sara was two years old at the time.

On the way to Taylor's place, I realize that neither parent ever gave Matty (or me) the appropriate "sex talk."

I seize the moment to give Matty some sisterly advice.

"You know, Matty, if you have any questions, you can always ask me anything."

"What kind of questions?"

"You know, about...dating. Or...whatever."

"Dating or whatever?" Matty laughs, "Well, this ought to be good. Sure, go for it."

"Well, I just...I mean, I know that you and Taylor are...a couple. Right?"

"Yeah. I guess."

"Okay, so, have you...you know?"

"Oh my God, is this the best you can do?"

I think about turning on the radio and forgetting the whole thing, but my stupidly strong sense of responsibility won't let me. "I just want to make sure you're being careful."

"You do know that getting preggers is impossible, right?"

"I'm not talking just about the physical part."

"Oh."

"Just...respect each other and listen to each other. Like, really listen. Okay?"

"You never even had a real relationship, so how do you know anyway?"

"I don't know. Instinct."

"Well, I have instincts, too," Matty says.

"I know that. But just in case yours are overshadowed by your mega powerful tween hormones, I thought I'd lend you some of mine."

This makes her laugh a little. Now that she's let her guard down, I figure it's my chance to inquire some more.

"Whatever the answer is to my next question, you should know that I love you no matter what, and I'm just curious, okay?"

Matty answers me before I can ask her anything, "I don't know," she says.

"You don't know what?"

"I don't know if I'm a lesbian or bi or straight. I don't know yet. Isn't that what you were going to ask me?"

"Yes."

"All I know is that Taylor makes me feel better about being me. He gets me and I get him. I don't care if people think it's weird."

"Good. That's good. I just...I want you to be happy."

"Yeah, me, too."

Taylor is waiting on the front porch, smiling and waving when we arrive. He really is a sweet kid and so lucky that he has such a supportive family. A family who's really there for him.

Matty leaps out of the car before I can come to a complete stop. She doesn't say goodbye as she slams the door shut.

I watch them happily embrace. I really want to be overjoyed for her, but my mind is having trouble wrapping around the fact that my fourteen-year-old sister has found love and I can barely find like. She doesn't care at all what people think, and I care way too much.

On my way home, I purposefully take Balboa because I know that Enzo and his boys sometimes shoot hoops at Balboa Park. I just want to look at him without him knowing that I'm there. If he can't see me, he won't talk to me. If he doesn't talk to me, he can't make me feel like an awkward, emotionally stunted freakazoid.

I see him. He's near the courts on a bench, watching his friends play. I park my car conveniently behind a big tree and turn the engine off. This is risky. If I'm busted, I'll have to come up with an excuse as to why I'm sitting in my car at the park by myself. But if he doesn't see me, this is a great opportunity to get to know him without actually...getting to know him.

Someone just sat down next to him on the bench. It's a girl. Even from this distance, I can tell that she's tall and beautiful with a perfect head of blonde hair. He just brushed some of that beautiful, perfect, blonde hair off her shoulders. This makes me self-consciously attempt to straighten my own messy head of hair with my fingers, which of course gets tangled up in it immediately.

I can't hear what they're saying, but apparently this beauty queen is also hilarious because now he's laughing hysterically. Oh my God, he just pulled her toward him and he...kisses her! A long, intense, movie kiss. They part only a few times in order to catch the occasional breath. One of Enzo's buddies yells some-thing at him, but he ignores him. He and this girl go at each other's faces, while I watch in shattered disbelief in the shadows. *If he has a girlfriend, why does he keep asking me out? Did he just meet her? Did he not really ask me out all of those times? Did I say no one too many times?*

Did I permanently screw up my Enzo opp?

Annie Wood

Another nod to e.e. cummings:

When words called, clouds are drifting above
And speaking isn't listening, and listening isn't
hearing
But silence is growing with every need
It's heard (yes, heard by caring) it's spoken.
So the breeze of the wind sings
So the sky smiles while colors shine
(So the sun and the moon share a cup of tea)

When every noise is made without a sound
And hearing is understanding and understanding is
believing
But questioning is normal and normal is doubting
Being; we are being: look (listen)at)to) me.
Now the butterfly flies as do you and do I
Now the owl asks who as we do why
(Now the sun and the moon are drinking; are drink-
ing)

When more than we have has been noticed has
been noticed And questioning is normal and normal is
feeling
But quiet not knowing is unaware is dying
It's spoken (all is heard all is know) o spoken.

All the birds swim in the sea All the fish float in the sky

(And the moon and the sun are one)

kinship

{kɪnʃɪp}
blood relationship
*the state of having common characteristics or a
common origin.*

My head is still reeling from the Enzo sighting this
morning. The girl he was with—who is she? Are they a
serious item? Does she know about me? What's there
to know about me? I keep thinking about her hair all
wavy and bright. It waved like the ocean and shone
like the sun. Basically, her head represented the most
beautiful parts of nature that any boy would find
irresistible. I'm not a boy and I find it irresistible. She
looked about twenty. Maybe that's what's going on
here. Enzo is twenty and technically, he shouldn't
really be chasing me in a romantic way since I'm
under age. I mean, sure, I'm a mature seventeen,
almost eighteen, but still, maybe it weirds him out. But
then why does he keep asking me out?

Enzo lives by himself in an apartment his uncle got
him. Must be nice to live solo. I'll bet his apartment is
sophisticated. He most likely has abstract art on the

walls and artsy coffee table books full of photos of Europe. I've always wanted to see his place. I wonder if I'll ever be invited over. Doubtful, if he's with the more appropriately aged hair model. Although, maybe the age thing is a non-issue, and maybe he was just kissing that girl on the park bench…because…hey…maybe it was a *goodbye kiss!*

I am so spinning right now.

***

I attempt to shake off the Enzo fantasies as I chop the veggies for tonight's family dinner. Grilled fennel and shiitake mushrooms as a side.

The salmon in now efficiently marinated, so I open up the preheated oven and pop it in. If you're wondering why I seem so skilled in the kitchen. It's because when mom went through her Cooking and Cleaning Juncture, The Food Network was on constantly. And I'm a damn good absorber of information. Everyone will be here soon and I really want this night to go well. We were never much of a "family dinner" type of family. With the exception of mom's cooking phase and the holidays, most nights we just grabbed whatever out of the fridge and went to our separate rooms, to our separate screens and just did our own separate things.

I do remember one time, though, when we all ate together. I was in the fourth grade, and an older girl in school was bullying me. She cornered me up against my locker after school and told me that if I didn't do her homework for her, she'd beat me up. She was about a foot taller and had more meanness in her than I could ever fake. I thought her meanness meant that she was tougher. I thought that there was no way that good (me) could conquer evil (her), even though it happens in the movies all the time. So, I agreed. I did her homework every day for three weeks, until the day I saw her pulling the same moves on someone else. I witnessed my bully corner another girl, younger than me, smaller than me. She bullied her to tears until the girl gave my bully, our bully, her backpack and ran away. The bully laughed as she went through the girl's pack, took a juice box out, and began to drink it. Then she tossed the pack into the trash.

I. Was. Livid.

Something inside of me burst. The injustice of it all! People can't treat people this way! This sort of thing can't keep happening! Not on my watch. Before I could think it all the way through, I ran full speed ahead and rammed my head into the bully's stomach, surprising the hell out of her. She fell right back into the trash. I leaned in real close to her shocked bully face and said, "Stop being an asshole. You're hurting people!" Then I grabbed the backpack out of the trash and the juice out of her hands. I thought about pouring the rest of the juice on her face, but then I figured I'd be treading too closely into Bully-land myself, so I just walked away.

For the entire week she was on her best behavior, not bothering me, or anyone else.

Later, when I told my parental units about it, they were so proud. Mom beamed, "My little girl is a spitfire!"

Dad applauded. "Atta girl! Never forget to speak your mind."

I miss that version of myself. She was so cool. At least for a day. Now, it seems that Matty may of have inherited all of the spitfire that was once lit inside me.

About two weeks after the trash can incident, it was around dinnertime and there was a knock at our front door. It was my former bully and her mom. My parents invited them in and we all sat on the sofa, listening to my former bully apologize for her bad behavior. She told us that her dad had just died and that things had been hard. She then looked over at her mom who said, "Not that that's an excuse, it's just…it's been a challenging time for us." They asked for my forgiveness. My parents invited them to stay for dinner. I remember watching my former bully— whom I was comfortable now calling by her given name— Tanya, and her mom as they ate, and my heart welled up with an ocean of sadness. I couldn't imagine not having a dad. Little did I know that just a few years later, I would feel a dad-less kinship with Tanya.

As it turns out, Tanya was never evil. She was just sad. I guess her sadness shape-shifted into anger and she didn't know what to do with it other than share it with unsuspecting classmates. That night, we all ate together as a family, plus two, and I started wondering why we didn't eat together more often. Why did it take outsiders to make us come together? I made a promise that when I grew up and had kids of my own, I would make family dinners mandatory.

***

I've been pleading with my mom for fifteen minutes now. "Mom, please. Everyone is sitting at the table. They're all waiting for you."

Mom covers her face under the bed covers like a three-year- old. "Go away!"

"You said you were okay with this," I remind her.

"I don't remember saying that."

"You may not remember saying it, but you said it."

"Am I supposed to just trust you?"

"Yes, you are. Come on, he just wants to see you."

"He's seen me plenty."

"He'd like to see you now. He asked about you."

She slowly removes the covers so I can just see her wide, blue-green eyes.

"What did he say?"

"He said…*how is she*?"

"And?"

"And…he also said…that he misses you," I lie and immediately feel guilty about it.

"He said that?" She is now sitting up, alert and all smiles.

I nod my confirmation; it feels less like less of a lie somehow.

"I need a hat."

She gets up and rushes toward her closet where there's an elaborate wardrobe from her acting days. She frantically pulls a dress off the hanger and holds it up against her body, modeling it for me. It's a black gown with rhinestones all over. Meant for the flashy red carpet, not our drab yellow kitchen.

"This one?" she asks.

"Um, well, it's kind of fancy, don't you think?"

"So am I." She quickly changes into it.

I zip up the back. We both stand in front of the mirror.

She's so tiny. Whenever I look at her, I have to fight the impulse to pick her up and rock her like a baby. She sits at her makeup chair and starts to put on her face. In less than ten minutes she went from sad-Mom-in-bed, to glamorous-woman-about-town. I'm part in awe of her and part annoyed. These split feelings I have about my own mother give me a headache. I rub my temples. She notices. "You think too much," she tells me.

"I'm fine." I make a mental note to not rub my temples in front of her again. "Let's go," I say.

I head out the door. She stays put. "Go where?"
"Downstairs. For dinner. Everyone's waiting."

"Oh, no. I'm not going downstairs." She says it in a way that implies the mere idea of traveling downstairs in her very own house is the most ludicrous thing a person could possibly suggest.

"But you're all dressed."

"They can come to me." She fluffs up her pillow and leans back, waiting for my response.

I don't respond. I often find myself in a perpetual game of tennis with people. They're always giving me their best serve and I don't always hit the ball back over the net. I just watch as the ball bounces on my side. Bounce. Bounce. Bounce.

I don't even go toward it. I just patiently wait until it stops bouncing and stops moving altogether. Usually I pick up the ball and place it carefully in its bucket with the rest of them. Everything in its place.

I go downstairs alone and calmly reach into the cupboards for serving trays.

"What are you doing?" Matty asks.

"We're dining in Mom's room tonight."

"That's lame," Matty says.

Bounce, bounce, bounce.

unconventional

[ənkən'ven(t)SH(ə)n(ə)l]
not bound by or conforming to convention, rule, or precedent; free from conventionality.

Matty and Sara sit cross-legged at the foot of the bed, quietly eating. Richard sits on my mom's little stool near her makeup nook, which makes him look like an uneasy giant, and I'm next to Mom, leaning back on the pillows that I stacked behind us. The room reeks of food with the rosemary salmon platter resting on a tray in the center of the bed, the garlic roasted veggies are in a bowl on the nightstand next to the mushrooms, and I went ahead and lit a few candles for atmosphere. This is the kind of setting that I suppose could be romantic if you're newlyweds that just moved into your first apartment, but for a family of five, it's crowded, awkward, and just plain odd.

"I've always loved that dress on you, Tessa," Richard finally says.

"It's new," she beams.

"No, I remember getting it for you for that charity dinner at my agent's condo. Remember? We have photos."

"Nope. Brand new," Mom repeats. "Everything that's old, is new again."

"I see," Richard nods, "It's a new moment, so it's a new dress."

"Exactly. In this moment, this dress is new." Mom's delighted to be having this particular conversation. That's one thing about Richard. When he wants to, he can be quite agreeable.

Sara giggles for no apparent reason.

Matty rolls her eyes for no apparent reason.

I refill everyone's glass of bubbly apple cider.

"Dinner is wonderful, Lauren," Richard says.

"My Lauren is an exceptional cook," Mom brags.

"Our Lauren," Richard corrects.

"Yeah, well, *everyone's* Lauren is an exceptional everything," Matty adds.

"That's not true," I say.

"Please. Name one thing you're not good at," Matty says.

"I don't know. Lots of things. I don't have a list. Besides, you're the one with the supersonic memory."

"It's called *semantic* memory. I can remember facts. It's not a big deal."

"Yes it is! Come on, Matty, tell us something we don't know," Richard says.

"I'm off duty."

"All my daughters are gifted," Tessa says.

"Even me, Mommy?" Sara asks.

"Of course," both Mom and Richard say at the same time.

"Jinx, you owe me a beer," Richard says.

We all stare at him.

"I meant a soda. You owe me a soda."

"No more beer for you then?" Mom asks.

"No more of any of that stuff. Ever again." He reaches into his pocket and pulls out his sobriety chip and hands it to her.

Mom takes it and inspects it. After a moment, she declares, "How wonderful. I'm happy for you. We must celebrate. Let's have a party!"

"Seriously?" Matty says. "He gets a party just because he's not doing something that he shouldn't be doing in the first place?"

"I like the idea of a party. I'll arrange it," I say.

We finish up our meal, but now there's excited chatter about the upcoming party and who to invite. My parental units are chatting it up like old times, which is really confusing since you'd think they'd have some issues to sort out. When Mom is like this, it's not so easy to see the bad parts. Her beauty and charm are lovely curtains that hang delicately over her madness and sadness. Her eyes are wide and alert, and she's all here in the room with us. In her fancy gown, in her glorious bedroom slash dining room kingdom, she appears to be in control of her thoughts and her mood, and if she should falter, I think Richard might actually know how to play along. I begin having fantasies and my mind daydreams itself to a summer camp where I find my identical twin and we plot and plan to get our parents back together again. If Lindsay Lohan can do it, how hard can it be?

By the time we get to molten chocolate lava dessert, even Matty has managed to thaw out some of her stone cold hostility. In fact, everyone seems light and happy as we all eat our dessert. Maybe it's just that it's difficult to be anything but happy when you're eating warm, melted chocolate.

Remembering that one time when you took me
sailing.

The wind kept howling TURN BACK.
But we made believe that we didn't understand.
We acted like we didn't speak Wind.
I was five and when I asked you why I had to wear
a life vest, you told me because my life meant every-
thing to you.
and the vest could save my life.
I didn't understand why you didn't wear a life vest.
Didn't your life mean everything to you?
You poured yourself another drink and winked at
me.
I thought you were sweet.
Because you are.
Sweet to me—
but now I see,
sour to yourself.
Like the sweet and sour chicken from the Chinese
restaurant we used to order take-out from.
It was hit and miss.
Like us.
The face in the mountain snarled at us.
But we turned our gaze away from the mountain.

Just a Girl in the Whirl

We acted like we couldn't see it.
You said, ... "Out of sight...out of mind."

diversion

[dih-vur-zhuh n, -shuh n, dahy-]
the act of diverting or turning aside, as from a course or purpose.

Our home is vibrating tonight with a large combo platter of laughter, music, and second chances. Luckily, Sara can sleep through just about anything, as long as I make sure to turn up her whistling dolphin sound machine. She's upstairs, as cozy as can be, after I read her six stories. That's two more than usual. I think she senses that we might be having some fun without her.

Matty brought Taylor over for the first time and everyone's been welcoming and not overly inquisitive about it. There's some of Richard's old friends and their significant others milling about. I found them on his Facebook page. Antonio and Maria both complimented me on the caprese on a stick appetizer. I baked Richard a sobriety cake. He seemed impressed and, even touched, when he read the icing inscription on it.

Congrats 1 year! We're so Proud.

He gives me a big hug. "You really are something, you know that? Listen, I want to ask you something."

"Sure. What?"

"I was wondering…what are your thoughts about me moving back in?"

"Well, I mean, it is your house."

"True."

"What does Mom think?"

"We haven't really discussed it yet. I wanted to run it past you first, since, you're obviously the one in charge here." He smiles at me. I smile at him.

Maria calls him from the other side of the room.

He turns back to me and says, "to be continued."

Mom is still upstairs putting the finishing touches on herself so she can make a grand entrance. She's big on grand entrances. I look around and notice that everything feels so…normal. This realization fills me up with a sense of calm. Everything might actually be okay.

Richard clinks the side of his bubbly apple cider glass with a spoon to get everyone's attention. People quiet down. He has the floor.

"I would like to take a moment to say thank you. Thank you to my friends who have welcomed me back after years of me…not being quite myself."

"You can say that again!" Antonio yells.

"You still owe me two hundred bucks!" yells another guy I don't know.

Everyone laughs.

"I'll write you a check, Stuart. I promise."

"Yeah, yeah," Stuart laughs.

"But mostly," Richard continues, "I need to thank my family who've allowed me to come back home after my regrettable actions."

I turn to look at Matty whose arms are crossed in front of her chest. Taylor uncrosses Matty's arms and puts Matty's hand in his.

Richard continues, "I want to thank my beautiful wife, who I intend to take care of, as promised."

Take care of? What does that mean. I wish mom would get downstairs already. I hate that she's missing this speech. As far as "I'm sorry" speeches without actually saying "I'm sorry" goes, this isn't half bad.

"Mostly, I would like to thank my beautiful daughters, Lauren, Matty, and Sara. Especially Lauren, who miraculously managed to keep everything together while I was away getting... myself together."

He winks at me. Everyone's looking at me and I'm not sure what to do or say so I just stand there smiling.

"A Toast." Richard raises his glass, everyone raises their glass.

"To Lauren!"

"To Lauren!" they all repeat.

Richard turns to me. "Just like your mother says, you're our perfect little fixer. Thanks, Sunflower."

There's a smattering of applause, then everyone goes back to their festivities.

Matty and Taylor rush over.

"Nice speech," Taylor says.

"Yeah. I can't believe it, but I think you finally got Dick to step up," Matty says.

"Maybe you can stop calling him Dick now."

"We'll see."

Taylor grabs a caprese on a stick. "These are crazy good."

"Thanks." I make a plate for myself and sit down. For the first time in...I can't remember how long, I feel relaxed. He's back. We're going to be us again.

"Uh oh," Matty says, nudging me.

"Was this supposed to be a costume party?" Taylor asks.

I look up and notice Mom at the top of the stairs. She's doing her full-on Norma Desmond performance—the floor-length gown, the diamonds and pearls in her updo, her ruby red lips. She holds a burning cigarette in one hand and a martini in the other.

159

"Hello, darlings. Welcome to my humble abode," she announces in a vague British dialect. Her huge, fake eyelashes look like black widows holding her eyes unnaturally open. Her expression is pained, just like Norma's.

"Tessa, sweetheart. You look positively divine." Richard bows theatrically. He then begins to applaud and everyone slowly, awkwardly, joins in.

Mom looks at everyone and concern washes over her face. She yells, "Get out! Or I shall call my servant!"

Everyone is quiet until Richard starts to crack up. He turns to his friends, "Don't worry. You can all stay. She's just quoting *Sunset Boulevard*."

I maneuver toward her quickly. "Mom, let's get you a plate." I guide her to the kitchen.

"Sweetheart, I never eat before a performance. You know that." She touches my face gently, "You have his nose. It's okay. It's a good nose." She looks around frantically. "Oh no. I forgot to order the champagne."

"No, Mom. It's a sobriety party. It's dry."

"Dry? How dreadful."

"You shouldn't drink on your meds anyway. If you're even taking them. Oh, Mom, what am I going to do with you?" I say, mostly to myself.

"I think he wants to come back," she whispers like she's my classmate sharing High School gossip.

"Would you want that? For him to move back in?"

She shrugs and gets that faraway look in her eyes again. Matty comes running in announcing, "Your boyfriend's here."

"A boyfriend!" Mom claps excitedly.

"No...he's not...but, wait—he's here?" My mind starts spinning on overdrive.

Why would he be here? Is he alone? Did he come to see me? Maybe his uncle invited him. Before I have time to run to the bathroom to look in the mirror for a once-over, Enzo is in the kitchen, reaching into his backpack and pulling out a bottle of vodka.

"Let the party begin."

"I'll say." Mom claps even harder now as she makes a beeline for the booze.

I intercept. "Not a good idea."

She shrugs again. "Fine by me. I dance better when I have my wits about me anyway." She glides off back to the party, which leaves me alone with Enzo.

"Actually, this is a dry party, so maybe you can put that back in your backpack?"

"Well, a few sober buzz kills shouldn't ruin it for the rest of us." He twists off the top and swigs. He then holds it out for me.

"No, thanks."

"Right. I figured."

"What's that supposed to mean?" I say, trying not to sound too offended or prudish.

"It's just, you're so perfect, so I pretty much figured you don't drink. You probably don't even drink coffee. Like the Amish."

"I'm not perfect and I'm not Amish."

"Good," he says.

"Good," I say.

He takes another swig. He's managed to piss me off which somehow makes me feel brave so I ask pointedly,

"Where's your girlfriend?"

"What girlfriend?"

"The one from the park."

"Have you been spying on me, you naughty, naughty girl?" he teases.

"No. I just happened to be driving by."

"Well, Enzo doesn't do girlfriends."

I usually hate it when people refer to themselves by their own name. That whole speaking in the third person thing is so douchey, but maybe he did it ironically and I just didn't get it.

"Oh," I say.

He grabs an uneven-looking appetizer off of a tray. "No, those didn't make it. The good ones are already out."

"Calm down. Wow, these are damn good."

"Yes, they taste the same but they look—"

"—Yeah, I heard you, they're not the 'good ones.' That's cool, 'cause I think good is totally overrated." He moves closer to me.

I can feel the heat building up from my toes, spreading all over my body, and I can't think of a thing to say or do. I know that this is the moment when Enzo kisses me for the first time, so I close my eyes...

But, instead of a kiss, I hear him take another swig of vodka. I open my eyes, feeling like a complete idiot, but he's not even looking at me, which hurts on one level but on another level, it does make the whole thing a tad less humiliating.

That's when I hear something break in the living room. I rush in and see Mom dancing with Richard, her champagne glass shattered all over the floor. But I'm so hypnotized by seeing my parents looking into one another's eyes, holding each other close as they sway back and forth, I don't rush to clean up the broken glass. I catch Matty also noticing. We both stand, frozen, watching.

Finally the song ends, and I come in with a broom to gather up the glass.

Mom kisses me on the forehead. "Everything is as it should be, my little pea." She rhymes when she's happy. She's no longer Norma Desmond, she's my sweet, rhyming mom in the arms of her getting-his-shit-together-husband. I'm thinking I might have a future in party planning.

"I'm going to get more sparkling apple cider," I hear Richard tell her, "and a new glass for you."

Mom giggles like a school girl and Richard leaves for the kitchen. She tells me, "He wants to stay, Lauren."

"I know, Mom. How do you feel about that?"

"He says he wants to take care of me."

Mom pulls me close and we dance in the living room to Frank Sinatra singing about how he's got the world on a string. Mom joins in singing along with Frankie and she twirls me around with all of our guests watching and smiling.

I look over Mom's shoulders and I can see Enzo's profile in the kitchen. He's talking to my dad. I feel guilty for not fully enjoying my bonding moment with my happy-for-now Mom, but all I want is to be the person Enzo is talking to. Matty surprises me by grabbing Taylor's hand and joining us on the dance floor. She's usually way too "cool" for this sort of display of fun, but, here she is. My usually angst-ridden little sis is smiling.

Mom turns to Taylor and says, "I like your tie. You're a very debonair young man."

Taylor blushes and grins so large I think his face might crack.

A few other guests have joined us now and everyone is singing along with Frankie. My dad is in the kitchen with Enzo.

Not sure what they have to say to each other, but who cares? Everyone is happy. That's all I ever wanted.

A little while later I head upstairs to check on Sara. I half expect her to have made her way downstairs by now, stuffed rabbit in tow. I slowly open her door and see my adorable baby sis sleeping adorably. I start to head back into the kitchen to recreate that almost kiss with Enzo when I'm distracted by a sound coming from my room. I make my way to the door and the sounds start to become more familiar. Holy crap. *Sex sounds are originating from my room.* This is creepy. I mean, I'm glad people are enjoying themselves at my party, but I'd really rather they didn't do the enjoying on my bed. They all have their own grown-up homes to do this sort of thing in. I think about walking away, but the curiosity gets the better of me. I slowly open the door just to have a peek at which rowdy party goers are sullying my bed. I see Maria's long, black hair and her naked back as her body rides some lucky guy. She arches her back and I now see the face of that lucky guy and everything in me freezes.

fragmentize

*[**frag**-muh n-tahyz]*
to break into fragments; break (something) apart.

"Lauren!" Richard jumps up, covering his bare body with my bed sheet. Maria scurries off to my bathroom, embarrassed.

"Dad?"

He pulls up his shorts and comes at me, reaching his arms out in a plea, "I'm sorry, Lauren, ...it's just..."

I can smell the vodka on his breath.

"You've been drinking? *At your sobriety party?*"

"I know, I screwed up...but...please...listen..."

I don't want to hear one more excuse from him that he will try to pass off as a "reason." This is not how a father should behave.

THIS.

IS.

NOT.

OKAY.

"NO!" I scream as I run out of my room and down the stairs.

My face must be beet red because Matty gets one look at me and runs over to me, "Lauren, what happened?"

I zoom past her and into the kitchen. There's no Enzo in sight.

Matty's right behind me now. She sees me searching and says, "Enzo left about a minute ago."

I push past her. I can hear Frankie now singing at us that *The Best is Yet to Come* and I don't believe him. I look back at my mom, who is sitting on the recliner, pretending to smoke her cigarette, and laughing too hard at something Antonio said. I bolt out the front door and I can see Enzo in the not-too-faraway distance. I stop myself on the front stoop. I take a deep breath and I think about how badly I want to scream at him for bringing booze to a party that's supposed to celebrate the fact that someone has abstained from booze, but instead I shout, "Hey!"

He stops. He turns back.

"Where are you going?" I ask him.

"Nowhere," he says.

I leap off the front stoop and make my way toward him. "Good. Me too."

bolt

[bohlt]
a sudden dash, run, flight, or escape.

Me and Enzo are swinging on the kiddie swings at the park. It's midnight, so we're the only humans present and there's one repetitive owl in a faraway tree. I find the owl to be kind of calming. Or maybe that's just the vodka talking.

I take swigs too, just like Enzo. Gone are the days of a Lauren who didn't drink. This is the new, bad-ass Lauren, who knocks back vodka with sailor swigs. I feel like a prisoner that just took advantage of an explosion that disintegrated the prison walls.

"Who, who who," says the owl.

"Me, me, me," I reply.

This causes Enzo to laugh, which causes him to spit vodka in my face.

"Ewww."

"Sorry, you're just too much." He laughs.

"Really?" No one has ever said I was too much before. But I usually tell myself that I'm not enough.

"I didn't realize you were so funny. And cool. A firecracker."

This creates a singing impulse in me that I can't deny. I stand up on the swing and belt me out some Katy Perry...singing about fireworks and colors bursting and making them go, *ahh, ahh, ahhh...*

"You have the voice of an angel," Enzo says sarcastically as he pulls me down from the swing. "Please don't ever sing again."

"Fuck you," I say.

"Whoa. I've never heard you curse before. I didn't know you could do that."

"Everyone has equal access to curse words."

"It's just so not like you."

"Well, this is the new Lauren. And the new Lauren is known for singing in parks at midnight, drinking vodka, and dropping F bombs."

"She's known for it?"

"Yeah. She's legendary."

"Wow."

"Damn straight, wow."

I grab the vodka from Enzo and have another gulp. The look on his face is a mishmash of expressions I don't recognize on him. He's usually so glib, expertly wearing that patented, confident, lopsided grin. I'm buzzing hard and I don't care what's on his stupid, beautiful face. I just know that I desperately want to taste it.

"And the new Lauren...the new Lauren takes whatever she wants." I grab onto Enzo's t-shirt and pull him close. I bring his lips to mine and kiss him deeply. I pull him onto the sand below the swings and climb on top of him.

"I think new Lauren is awesome," he says between kisses.

"You do?"

Enzo pulls away from me for a moment and gets a serious look on his face that I've never seen before. "Actually," he says, "I've always thought that about you."

"Seriously?"

"You're so together. And the way you are with your little sisters, and how you always take care of everything and everyone all the time. I can barely keep my own shit together, but you...you take care of everyone's shit. It's awesome." Enzo looks down on at the ground. "You deserve something good."

I pull him close to me and whisper into his ear, "You're good."

"No. I'm not."

"Well, maybe I'm sick of good." I kiss him and he kisses back. We roll around for a moment, picking up from before he got all serious with all those words. I feel a vibration in my front pocket. "I'm vibrating," I say.

"Yeah, I know, me too," he says.

"No, literally." I push myself off Enzo and I take out my phone. It's a text from Matty.

> *mom locked herself in her room.*
> *dad is gone.*
> *sara is crying.*
> *WHERE R U?* 😠

I put the text out of my mind and let myself get lost in Enzo. He tastes like a spice I've never had, and he smells better than any boy I've ever smelled. Not that I go around smelling boys, it's just…he's so sexy I can't think straight. He takes of his t-shirt and in an attempt to prevent myself from gawking at his perfect abs, I busy myself by pulling off his jeans but I forget about his shoes, so the jeans get stuck at his feet. He reaches for my pants and I really don't want to break the mood but…

"Do you have a condom?" I whisper in a way I pray is sexy and cool.

"Yeah, at my place."

"Should we go there, then?"

"No, don't worry, I'll pull out."

"You sure you don't have one in your pocket?"
"Shhh…" he whispers, "trust me."

I sit up and straighten my top. "Enzo, no, we can't."

He sits up and stares at me.

Two, four, six, I count the freckles on his nose.

"Lauren, come on, yes, we can." He pulls me back on top of him.

I can feel the blood begin to boil inside my chest. I've gone this far and now I'm stopping. What will he think of me? "It's just…I really don't want to take the risk," I tell him.

"Life is all about risk," he says.

I push him off and stand up. I start dressing all the parts that have come undone. I'm feeling out of sorts.

I'm alone in a park at midnight at a park with a boy that I think I know, but do we ever really know a person, and oh my god, what if he doesn't take no for an answer? I'll fight him. I could do that. Oh shit, what have I gotten myself into? I'm so stupid.

"Maybe some other time when we're more pre-pared," I say calmly.

"Okay, fine. Just come back here. We can do other stuff," he says.

I start walking away. "I'm going home."

He attempts to get up, but the jeans are still trapped on his sneakers and he trips, falling on his face. "AHHH!"

I look back. He hit his nose on a rock! The rock is bleeding! Wait, that makes no sense. Too. Much. Vodka.

"You're bleeding!" I rush back to him and help him sit up.

He smiles at me. "A little pain is worth it if it gets you to stay."

I help him stand and pull up his jeans. I stuff some Kleenex in his nose and we head back to the house.

On our walk back, he leans heavily on me and mutters, "There's a twenty-four-hour liquor store near my apartment. We can get condoms there."

"I think that ship has sailed."

"No, no. We can still sail! I want to sail!"

"How much did you have to drink, anyway?" I ask.

He shrugs. "Just my traveling vodka." He holds up an empty pint. He shared some with me, and I guess some with my dad, so why is he so trashed?

"And then of course I had my pre-game-home-vodka with a couple of extra goodies."

"Extra goodies?"

"Yeah, you know, a little Vicodin, a little Ativan, and my buddy's ADHD meds."

***

We finally reach my mom's car. I gently place him in the backseat, trying to be as quiet as possible so no one inside the house hears us.

"Do you remember where you live?" I ask him.

He mumbles his address right before he passes out.

As I drive past my house, I glance inside and it appears as if no one is home. Looks like the party's over. Then I look over my shoulder at my blacked out Prince Charming. He's snoring like a grizzly bear with sleep apnea.

Yep, the party's definitely over.

Annie Wood

I will
save,
fix,
heal you.
Except that I can't.
Why do I try?
Reasons like confetti fall from the sky.
Maybe if I think faster, I'll remember.
Maybe if I think slower, I'll realize.

Will it always be like this?
Does it have to always be like this?

ruminate

[roo-muh-neyt]
to meditate or muse; ponder.

It's 8:03 a.m. and I've been AWOL for exactly eight hours and twenty-three minutes. Since Enzo was obliterated, there was no hooking up. Or kissing. Or spooning. Or laughing. Or talking. Or...anything. Anything at all.

When we got to his place, I fished the keys out of his back pocket and, with the help of my body as his walking stick, managed to get him into his apartment. I changed the Kleenex in his nose and placed him in his bed, on top of the covers. I decided to leave his clothes on since undressing a comatose boy felt kind of gross. I found a blanket and draped it over him.

His apartment was practically empty with just a tiny love seat posing as a sofa, and two crates as a makeshift coffee table. He has a fake plant in the corner that, in spite of its fakeness, still looked like it needed to be watered. His apartment wasn't even trying to be sunny.

I slept, or sort of slept, on the sofa. My mind was flooded with what ifs.

What if Mom drowns in the fountain?

What if Dad dies in a drunk driving accident?

What if Matty and Taylor runaway together and end up on the streets?

What if Enzo is an addict?

What if when Enzo wakes up, he no longer likes me?

My restless sleep was also partly because of my phone blowing up. Texts from Matty all through the night.

2:20 a.m.

☡

3:12 a.m.

moms blaring THE SMITHS! ☹

3:47 a.m.

this is sooooo not like u!

4:11 a.m.

dads passed out. ☠

5:02 a.m.

im still up. txt me bck…

6:13 a.m.
taylor thinks im obsessing. told him that was ur job.

6:39 a.m.
srsly. im worried. at least tell me ur alive… 😫

She has a point. I mean, if Matty took off in the middle of the night and was gone all night long, I'd freak. I finally respond.

8:03 a.m.
I just need a break, k?

I wait a few minutes for a response. None comes. I try again.

8:07 a.m.
k?

I can hear Enzo stirring in his bed. Should I make him breakfast? Or is that too "mom like." Guys don't like that. Wait, maybe they do like that. How the hell am I supposed to know what guys like? Coffee. I think he likes coffee. Maybe I can do that.

***

I find my way into the kitchen and go through his cupboards, which are bare, except for a family-sized bag of barbecue Lays and liquor store onion dip. Maybe I'll have better luck with the fridge. Beer, beer, and more beer. I try the freezer. One half-filled tray of ice and another pint of vodka. Does he really survive on this stuff? Then I remember that he's been pretty much on his own since he was seventeen. Ever since his parents died, he's only had his Uncle Antonio to look after him. Antonio isn't a bad guy or anything, but he's not exactly warm and fuzzy, either. He yells at Enzo in Italian a lot. But maybe he's yelling positive, motivational type stuff. I don't know, I don't speak Italian. Antonio did give Enzo a job at the restaurant and this apartment to live in, though. But by the looks of things, I don't think anyone ever showed him *how* to live. Then again, I'm not sure what actual direction I've been given either, and I have two living parents. Technically. Anyway, all of this just means that Enzo really needs some looking after. And that's my jam.

Matty finally texts back.

8:15 a.m.

Nice.

"Hey," Enzo mutters as he drags himself into the kitchen, looking like a hot mess.

I wonder if he's still drunk. "Hey. I was going to make you breakfast, but…"

"Yeah, I forgot to go shopping." He opens up the fridge. Then he opens up the vodka bottle and has takes a swig. "Hair of the dog," he tells me.

"Oh. Yeah. Totally." I smile, trying my best to be chill and not in shock that he's throwing back vodka in the AM. I mean, here we are alone in his apartment and for once I have no place where I need to be, or at least no place where I'm willing to be.

There's a bed here. There are condoms here. My crush is here, half naked, standing right next to me. This is my moment.

"Hey," he says again.

"Hey," I say back.

"Sorry if I freaked you out last night." He leans in close.

He smells like musk and vodka and like my chance for a second first time.

"I don't freak out so easily," I tell him.

"Good to know. 'Cause I can be a real idiot sometimes."

"You're not an idiot."

I look into his bloodshot, dreamy eyes. We pick up from where we left off, pre-nosebleed. He leads me into his bedroom, kissing me all the while. I'm giddy with excitement and nerves, and dreams of our future. I remind myself to stay in this moment so I don't miss a thing.

***

A half an hour later, we're lying in bed and I'm leaning on Enzo's bare chest. I'm curling his tiny, baby fine chest hairs with my finger while he stares at his iPhone. He's watching a YouTube video of a kitten taking a bubble bath. He seems happy, but I don't know if he's happy because of what we just did, or because kittens taking bubbles baths make him happy. I feel...different. Way different than my first, first. This time I feel more grown up. I've witnessed this moment in my mind so many times-being here in Enzo's arms. I finally got exactly what I wanted.

So why do I feel so alone?

"Let's go out for breakfast," I suggest.

"Nah, I'm good." He doesn't look up from his phone. "These cats are hilarious."

I had no idea this guy had such a love of kittens. That's so cute. I guess. I brush his hair out of his eyes and stare at him. I don't feel self-conscious about staring at him anymore, because, well, we're close now. Besides, he's not really paying attention.

I begin to think of all of the ways I can make things better. When I'm Enzo's official girlfriend, I will always make sure there's real food in the cupboards, and fresh produce in the fridge, and something to drink other than booze. In fact, I'll probably be instrumental in getting him to cut back on the alcohol. And once I move in, I will, for sure, tidy up the place. Hang some pictures on the wall. Maybe a framed photo of us frolicking on the beach or something. A super-sized photo with an antique wood frame hung over the new, beautiful sofa we will purchase together from one of those fancy furniture stores on Melrose.

"Okay," I say. "How about we go see a movie or something?"

"Sorry, can't today. Maybe some other time." He gets up and heads for the bathroom. He leaves the door open as he pees.

"I can go pick up some food and we can just stay in," I suggest.

"I can't hear you over the piss!" he yells. As if that wasn't delightful enough, he then lets one rip before he flushes.

"Oops!" He laughs.

I wonder if this is what living with a boy is like 24/7. Well, I suppose passing gas is a natural thing. I can just pretend this particular natural thing didn't happen during what should be our afterglow.

He climbs back into bed and reaches toward me. I move in to kiss him, but he moves past me as he reaches for his phone. "I got some chips in the cupboard if you're hungry," he says, then reopens his YouTube app. Now he's watching the video where the cats are freaked out by cucumbers.

He cracks up. "Cats are ridiculous!"

Yeah, that's not the only thing that's ridiculous. I thought boys his age were supposed to be insanely horny. How is he not all over me right now? Maybe it's me. Maybe I should brush my teeth. I jump out of bed and head into the bathroom so I can rub some toothpaste onto my gums. He's acting so distant right now, but I'm sure it'll get easier the more we hang out. I just need to be patient.

I find some toothpaste and use my finger as a brush. I spit the toothpaste out and rinse my mouth. I'm about to open the bathroom door to make my way back to my guy, but I'm stopped by the sound of a new voice. A girl's voice. It says, "Hey, baby."

"Babe. Hey. I thought I was going to meet you at your place," Enzo nervously tells the girl he calls "'babe.'"

"I decided to come here first," Babe says.

"Oh, cool," Enzo says.

"Get dressed. I'm hungry," Babe says.

I pull the door open a crack to get a glimpse of her. I catch her profile. Her perfect face is elegantly framed by her wavy, blonde locks.

"I'll wait outside. It stinks in here." She leaves and I can hear Enzo scrambling to get dressed.

I step out of the bathroom and wait. I wait for Enzo to tell me that he's not really into Babe and that he's just getting dressed so he and I can spend the day together. I'm ready for him to tell me all the things that will make this right.

"I guess you heard Sherrie," he says sheepishly.

Babe has a name.

"Is she your girlfriend?"

"Yeah, she is."

"But, I asked you if she was your girlfriend when I saw you that day at the park."

"You did?"

"You said, 'Enzo doesn't do girlfriends.'"

"Oh. Yeah, that sounds like me."

"Well, is she or isn't she?"

"Yeah, it's just…I need, like a little break from her sometimes. Sherrie can be real intense."

"So I was your little break?"

"Yeah. But, in a good way. A good little break." He shoves his head through the hole in his hoodie, then rushes at me and kisses me on the forehead—you know, the way you'd kiss your little sister. I feel like I'm going to throw up.

"I had fun," he says. "Thanks," he adds.

"Thanks? Did you just thank me?" I ask hurriedly putting on my shirt.

"Hey, Lauren, you can leave whenever, no rush," he tells me as he walks away.

I quickly pull on my pants and yell, "HOLD THE FUCKING PHONE!"

"Umm…I'm not on the phone."

"It's an expression. Now shut the door and listen to me!"

He shuts the door. "Why are you so mad right now?" he asks.

"Seriously? Are you dense?"

"If that means an idiot, then yeah, I already told you that," he says.

"Yes, I'm mad. I'm mad because you can't just decide that someone is *a little break!*

"Okay."

"Okay? That's all you have to say right now?"

"I should really get going. Maybe you can just text me all of this."

"No. This is NOT part of the plan!"

"What plan?" he asks.

"The plan I've had since I was fourteen years old. The plan that you'd finally notice me and you'd invite me over to your grown-up apartment and it would be warm and romantic and our connection would be undeniable, like The Fitzgeralds, only without the crazy."

"The who?"

"My God! Read a book!"

"I thought you said you don't freak out so easily," he says.

"Well, I take it back. Sometimes a person needs to freak out."

"That's true. I totally agree with that."

"Don't agree with me right now! I'm pissed at you!"

"Oh, okay. Sorry."

He stands there, looking lost in his own home. "Lauren, I'm not trying to be a jerk here, I thought you just wanted to have some fun."

"*This* is fun?" I ask him.

"Well, no, not this part. Definitely not this part," he says.

"You gave vodka to my sober Dad. Now you're about to dump me to go back to your girlfriend who you just cheated on with me. My life has been a nonstop train wreck and you were supposed to be my relief from all of that. This was supposed to fix everything."

Enzo shrugs, looking like a lost, stupid boy puppy. He says, "Oh, um...sorry?"

I push past Enzo's stunned face and sad apartment.

I pause for a moment and then turn back and say, "and get some real fucking furniture!"

I slam the door.

It was my very first door slam.

And it felt damn good.

Things to Know:

You have enough.

You are doing enough.

You are enough.

(Please make a note of it.)

Text from Matty.

12:37 p.m.

dick moved in

exhale

*[eks-**heyl**, ek-s**eyl**]*
to emit breath or vapor; breathe out.

Is it against the law to drive and cry at the same time? It should be, because I can barely see the road. Realizing the truth about Enzo makes me feel so naive. I pull into a parking structure because I really shouldn't be driving.

I'm walk-crying up Ventura Blvd, which seems safer, but way more exposed. I can't believe I put all that energy into making all of those future plans into a boy who, as it turns out, I didn't really know.

Plus, I abandoned my family when they needed me.

Just like my father.

And I'm acting so crazy.

Just like my mother.

"Watch where you're going!" a homeless woman yells as I almost trip over her.

"Sorry."

I keep walking, unsure of where I'm walking to. Or where I'm walking from. I just keep moving. I look back at the homeless woman. She looks to be about my mom's age. I wonder about her family. Do they know where she is? Did they try to help her? I read somewhere that 25% of the homeless people in America have some sort of mental illness. I wonder that if they were able to get the right help, if they'd still be on the streets.

I'm not sure what I should do with this long, empty day ahead of me. I used to dream about this sort of thing; having a full day all to myself so I could write and...just...be.

I notice a stationary store and I stop to look in the window. My eyes catch sight of a beautiful, paisley bound journal. It's love at first sight.

***

I've been writing feverishly in my new journal for hours. I take a break to stretch in this scuzzy hotel room that I checked into. It's all I could afford with the cash I found in my jeans pocket, so here I am. My stomach is a bit queasy over the ick-factor of the hotel floors. I put down a towel and do a couple of downward dogs. But now I'm obsessing about the towels and wondering how often they wash them. Still, there's a little wooden desk, a squeaky bed, and a bathroom, and all those things are mine, all mine, for the night. I was kind of surprised when the front desk didn't ask for my ID or ask my age or anything at all. Well, no, that's not true. The lady at the counter did ask if I was paying in cash, and if I was planning on paying the "hourly rate." Hourly? Why would I do that? Anyway, I took out my cash and she handed me the key, and that was that.

The surround-sound-ear-splitting-sex-noises was off-putting at first, but I eventually managed to tune it out so I could write. Although, I'm surprised that the moans and groans seemed to go on and on with no end. I have noticed that the pitch often changes, and when I hear some words, the voices sound different. It's like there's a break in the activity, and then new noises begin again from entirely new people. This keeps happening about every hour at this hotel.

Ohhhhhhh. Hourly rate. Got it. Duh.

***

I'm staring at my phone at the website for The Write Stuff writers retreat. My submission material is all ready to send, writing samples, the filled out application, it's all there. All I have to do is hit the submit button. But what if I do submit and I don't get in because I'm not good enough? And what if I do submit and I get accepted? Could I really leave everyone for an entire year? Shouldn't I wait until my dad gets clean and my mom gets balanced? When will that be?

I get a text from Carlie.

hey. i know u wont answer. but, hey anyway.

Three years ago, when Carlie stopped by my house, unannounced, it just so happened to be two days after Richard left. Mom had locked herself in her bedroom, Sara was in dire need of a nap, so she was crying her brains out and Matty was burning something that smelled like death in the oven. Also, I was freaked out because I had an algebra exam the next day and I hadn't even studied. My entire world was falling apart and I really wanted to tell Carlie all about it, but I didn't. I was too ashamed. Carlie had this amazing mom she could talk to about anything. Carlie had tons of family and friends to help her and support her without her even needing to ask. I didn't want Carlie to feel sorry for me. Plus, I had just seen a movie where this kid got taken away from her home because of her neglectful parents, and I didn't want that to happen to us. So, when Carlie came over that day and showed up at the front door, I shut the curtains and turned off the lights and made everyone pretend like we weren't home. When I saw her in school the next day, I pretended like everything was fine. After that, our friendship was never the same.

After graduation, I stopped returning her texts altogether.

But now, now...I get out my phone and text:

hey. wanna hang out?

She responds within a nanosecond.

YES!

decipher

*[dih-**sahy**-fer]*
to discover the meaning.

We're drinking Starbucks green tea lattés as we sit on the Mulholland Drive lookout bench. I can feel Carlie staring at me while I take in the expansiveness of my city. This view has been in a ton of movies and TV shows, and I can see why. Thousands of toy houses on their tiny, toy hills. The baby blue sky and the cotton candy clouds. There's a garden of leafy, green trees, all sorts of varieties, covering the surrounding hills. I wonder why I've never sat here before. But the only view Carlie seems interested in right now is my face.

"Stop staring, weirdo," I say.

"You're the weirdo, weirdo." Carlie hugs my shoulders. "I just can't believe it's really you."

"Yeah, me neither."

She lets go of my shoulders and looks at me. "Are you okay?"

"Everything's fine." I hear my own answer and I don't agree with it. Not anymore. "Actually…that's not true. Everything is so not fine."

I tell Carlie everything.

The facts: Dad leaving the premises, Mom leaving her senses, Matty's anger, taking care of a toddler.

The feelings: overwhelmed, exhausted, pressured to keep up a façade. I even tell her about my OCD tendencies and my dream to attend the writers retreat. I tell her all about my bathtub poems and how I desperately wish to escape from all the responsibilities that were heaped on my shoulders, and how I miss being a kid.

I begin to cry. Again. Only now it feels like more of a release cry than a regret cry.

Carlie puts her arm back around my shoulders. "My mom always says that no one gets a prize for getting through life solo. Life's a team sport. We need to ask for what we need."

I hear another text come in. Matty sent a selfie of her, Sara, Richard, and Mom all at the kitchen table with the caption:

someone is missing.

"Aww, that's sweet," Carlie says.

"Matty doesn't usually do sweet," I say.

"Well, maybe she's maturing or something."

"Yeah, maybe."

"It's nice that they're all together," Carlie says as she looks at the photo more closely. Carlie's never met her dad. Her mom was a "free spirit," and as such, forgot to get the name of the guy who knocked her up sixteen years ago. Looking at Carlie now as she stares at the photo on my phone, I can feel a sense of longing for what's missing in her own life. It makes me appreciate what I do have. As messy as it is, at least we're all together, more or less. And because of that fact, I guess, maybe, there's still hope.

"Together," Carlie repeats the word, more to herself than to me.

"I should go home. No, actually, I want to go home," I say.

"Home is good." Carlie smiles.

I guess I should have paid hourly for the hotel after all.

strive

[strahyv]
to exert oneself vigorously; to try hard.

I've barely set the keys down and Sara grabs my leg screaming, "Lauren. You're home!"

Mom whirls over and covers me in kisses. "My baby. I'm so happy you're okay."

Richard is right behind her. "Kiddo, my God, you had us worried."

Even Matty gets in on the action, sans hug. "Glad you're back, bossy-butt."

"Thanks," I say, grinning. I've been gone for less than twenty-four hours, but based on their reactions, you'd think I just returned from war.

I look at my dad. He looks better than he did the other night. He may have had a shower. He holds a mug of coffee in his hands and sheepishly points to his luggage that rests near the sofa.

"I'd like to…if it's okay…with you…I just…the thing is…"

"Feel free to finish a sentence. I'll wait," I say.

"Your father is back. On a trial basis," Mom says in her calm, cool, and collected voice. I like her in that voice.

Much to my surprise, Grandma Gayle emerges from the kitchen with a tray of cookies.

"Wipe the astonishment off your face, Lauren. The cookies are store bought," Grandma says.

Everyone grabs a cookie while I try to put the pieces together.

"Grandma's going to help out for a while," Matty says.

"She is?" I ask.

"I called her," Matty says.

"Seriously?" I say.

"Grandma is going to live here!" Sara cheers.

"She's what?"

"Help me in the kitchen," Matty says as she pulls me away.

"Help you in the kitchen? Since when do you do anything other than eat in the kitchen?"

Matty and I are alone in the kitchen. She hops up on the counter and grins. "I told them that you refused to come home unless everyone agreed to some changes."

"And they just went along with it?" I ask, amazed.

"Mom was really scared that you'd run away and join a cult."

"A cult?"

"She saw a documentary on Netflix about it."

"Well at least she turned on the TV," I say.

"Progress, right?" Matty smiles.

"This is all so crazy," I say.

"Oh, and the best part, Dad said he's committed to making real changes."

"Did you just call him Dad?"

"I guess I did. Anyway, Sara made me promise to get you to come home, and since you weren't responding to my texts, I had to think of something. So, I called Grandma and demanded that she come home and deal with her son."

"You demanded?"

"I demanded."

"Wow."

"Yeah, that demanding thing, I highly recommend it." Matty walks over to the fridge where there's a piece of paper secured by a quote magnet I've never seen before. She comes back with the magnet and the paper and places them both on the counter.

"What's this?"

She hands me the magnet and I read it out loud. "

Matty smiles and nods knowingly, but I'm totally lost. I read the magnet and then ask Matty, "What works if you work what?"

"It's a slogan," Matty says. "They have like a million of them. One day at a time, Live and let Live, Let go and let God...They really love their slogans."

"Who's they?

She pushes the paper toward me. It's a list of nearby AA meetings. "I took the liberty of logging onto your computer and reviewing your history," Matty says.

"That's a violation of my privacy," I say.

"You were missing. I had to do whatever it took to find you."

"I wasn't missing. I left."

"Semantics. Anyway, I saw that you searched for local AA meetings. I printed out the list and Grandma drove Dad to a meeting this morning. Apparently, they let you back in if you screw up."

"So then, he agreed to keep going?"

"That's the only way Mom said he could stay. If he went to meetings."

"Mom made a rule?"

"Then she said that she's going to need to go back to her therapist and talk about possibly tweaking her meds."

"She said that?" I'm in shock that so much talking was going on between everyone. I didn't know they could do that.

"We had a family meeting. Don't worry, Sara was at a playdate, so she didn't have to hear any of it," Matty says proudly.

Communication? Family meetings? Playdates? Did I wander too far last night and fall through a portal into a parallel universe or something? This is not my family. My family doesn't deal with anything. This new family, they're dealing like a boss. This is crazy weird.

"Oh, and in case you're wondering, Mom and Dad are not back together or anything. At least not yet. Dad's sleeping on the couch."

"O-kaaaay," I say. I've never seen Matty like this. She's so...enthusiastic.

"Oh, I almost forgot. I ordered a pizza. Gluten-free crust, and I made a salad. We ate already, but I'll make you a plate." Matty opens the fridge and starts taking the food out.

"You made a salad?"

"You're going to have to snap out of this stupor, sis. I am capable of things. We all are," she says as she hands me a napkin and fork.

"I know that you're all capable. I just didn't know that you were all willing," I say.

"I had a lot of time to think last night while I stayed up waiting for you," she says.

"What about?"

Matty grabs a cherry tomato off my plate and pops it in her mouth. "Did you know that there was a Penn State study that found that by the time a kid reaches eleven, they've spent about 33% of their free time with their sibling?"

"No, I didn't know that," I say.

"I think that means that our siblings probably know us better than just about anyone, don't you?"

"Yeah, probably."

We look at each other for a while, not saying anything. Matty picks tomatoes off my plate as I eat my pizza slice. I can hear chatter in the other room. The chatter isn't fighting, it isn't frantic, and it isn't slurry, intoxicated chatter. It's nice to hear it in the distance, even though I can't make out what they're saying. It's nice to know we're all under the same roof tonight, and it doesn't feel like I'm sitting on top of a fault line. I don't think a quake is coming. At least not tonight.

Matty grabs another tomato off my plate. "Did you know that in the early fifteen hundreds, when tomatoes were first brought to Europe, people thought they were poisonous?"

"Really?"

"Yeah, at the end of the nineteenth century, rich Europeans used pewter plates, which had a real high lead content. So when they'd put sliced tomatoes—which has a high acid content—onto the plate, it would leech the lead and people got lead poisoning. They blamed the tomato and called it, 'the poison apple.' Matty pops the tomato into her mouth and smiles. It's been a long time since she offered up her knowledge like this without being asked.

"I didn't know that," I say, "thanks."

"Sure," she says standing up. "I guess we should get back in there."

Before we leave the kitchen Matty turns back to me and says, "Oh, by the way, since your follow-through really sucks, I went ahead and clicked the submission button for you for that retreat thingy."

My mouth drops open.

Matty smiles and says, "You're welcome."

Freedom is a state fair with rickety rides that could
fall apart while you're in mid-air.
You feel lucky when the ride is over and you-aren't
over.
So lucky that you get right back in line to do it all
over again.
There's whisky on the breath of the clown,
But there's cotton candy for dinner.
There's everything you want,
and don't want,
all in one place.
You can play the carnival games,
Even though they're all rigged.
You can listen to the live band,
Even if they sing off tune.
You can get crafty with
candles,
soap,
or
jam.
You can watch.
You can participate.
You can be afraid.
You can be overjoyed.
whatever it is that you choose to be…

Annie Wood

or not be…
it's all
up
to
you.

transfigure

*[trans-**fig**-yer or, esp.-**fig**-er]*
to change in outward form or appearance; trans-
form.

It's been one week under the new living arrange-
ments and Grandma Gayle, control freak that she is,
wasted no time in taking over. I woke up this morning
to find her rearranging the living room furniture.

I shoot her a puzzled look.

"Just making the space more livable, Lauren," she
replies to the puzzled look on my face. She then pushes
the loveseat toward the window.

"It's plenty livable as it is. We've been living here,
in this livable space, for a long time now," I tell her
pushing the loveseat back.

"I thought it could be better organized."

"Too much change will just freak everybody out," I
say.

"And by everybody, you mean you?" Grandma
Gayle says as she pushes the loveseat back.

"Matty and Sara prefer to face north when they
watch TV," I say, moving the loveseat again.

"Why?" she asks.

"What do you mean why?" I ask.

"Why do they prefer to face north when they watch TV?"

"I don't know. I never asked them."

"They've actually told you what positional preference they have when they watch television?" Grandma asks.

"They didn't have to tell me. I know them. I know what they like," I say.

Grandma shakes her head and snickers. "Yes, well, I predicted you wouldn't go for this. You're nothing if not predictable."

"I am not predictable!" I tell her, hating being told what I am.

"Of course you are. It's okay, dear. It's just how you are. Things have to be a certain way, and if they're not, your entire world comes crashing down."

"Stop talking about me like you know me, because you don't," I say.

"I could say the same thing to you about me," she replies.

"You're the adult. You're not supposed to make it difficult for your grandkids to get to know you!"

"Difficult? I've showed up every other week with a check and I always ask how you are and you always take my money and then shoo me away."

"You were just acting out of obligation," I say.

"Even if that's true, I still showed up, and do you know that you never, not once, invited me in?"

"I…I thought…you always seemed so busy."

"Busy? With what? Pilates? Book club? Shopping? I only said those things so you wouldn't think I was a sad, old woman and feel sorry for me. I hate it when people feel sorry for me," she says seeming more like me than I imagined.

"Yeah…me, too," I say, surprised.

Neither one of us knows what to say next. Grandma's facial expression gets tighter and her forehead crinkles. I think she might yell at me some more, but she doesn't. She takes a deep breath and says quietly, "I know that you don't think much of me."

"I never said that."

"You didn't need to say it."

"I never knew you wanted to come in," I say.

"Well, I'm in now." She almost smiles at me and I can see what she might have looked like when she was a little girl. A little sad. A little misunderstood.

She moves the loveseat back to its original spot and then looks at me like she wants to say something but she doesn't know what. At that moment, something inside me wiggles loose and vaporizes. What once felt like a solid brick at the bottom of my gut magically turns into…something light, like balsa wood. A wood that can float.

"No, let's put it back." I move the loveseat back to where she had it.

"Are you sure?" She asks.

"A little change might be good," I say.

***

Happy birthday to me! It's been thirty-seven days since that one night when I took that self-appointed time-out and, surprisingly, everyone is still in one piece. Although, I keep waiting for the other shoe to drop. But if it were to drop, I think I, or someone else, would catch it before it falls into an abyss.

Dream Lauren still leaves me poems, but I don't need to rush off to the tub to write in secret anymore. I'm an out-and-proud writer who writes at the kitchen table, in my room, in the backseat of a car, at the park. Turns out "a room of my own" is no longer limited to my bathroom. My room is now anywhere that I happen to be.

A few days ago, I got wind of Matty conspiring with Grandma about a surprise party for me and I nipped that in the bud. I opted for a family hike instead. So, that's where we are now, here in Runyon Canyon going up a steep hill, together.

"Come on, it's not like this is Everest!" I call back to Dad, who takes more breaks than Grandma.

"Your mother is putting you to shame," Mom laughs. That's one thing I missed most of all: Mom's laugh. Not that wild- eyed, loose cannon laugh, but her natural, real laugh.

"Chop chop, Richard. Don't be a baby," Grandma Gayle calls back.

"Can you all...please...cut a guy...some slack?" Dad manages to get out between breaths, "I haven't been to the gym since I've been back."

Matty's carrying Sara in a baby Bjorn, a gift from Grandma Warbucks. Taylor is by her side. When the hill isn't too steep, they hold hands.

"It's a brave, new world," Grandma says, smiling at Taylor. "You could change your mind, you know. You're so young," she tells him.

"I'd have to change more than my mind. I'd have to change my soul," Taylor replies.

That was heavy enough to shut Grandma up for a while. To Grandma's credit, she seems to be making an effort to get to know all of us. Plus, she drives Mom to doctor's appointments and Dad to his meetings. This idea that I can relax now has taken some getting used to.

"Happy birthday to you, happy birthday to you..." Mom starts to sing.

"That's okay, you don't need to sing to me."

Everyone joins in loudly. "Happy birthday dear, Lauren...happy birthday to you."

They all cheer and clap, and as other hikers pass by, they wish me a happy birthday.

"Thanks," I mutter.

Mom picks up a stick and holds it up to Dad as if to start a duel. Dad finds a stick and they fence for a moment, like two actor kids on their front lawn. The world is their stage again. I hope this show has a long run.

We finally reach the summit, which gives us all a burst of energy. I turn to Matty and ask her for the zillionth time, "So, are you sure you hit the submit button?"

"It's not like it was a moving target. I hit the button," she says.

"And they sent a confirmation email that they received it?"

"I literally forwarded you that email the first time you asked."

"Oh, yeah. Right. You did."

"Is it getting hotter?" Grandma asks, looking flushed. She starts to wobble a bit.

Matty and I move closer.

"Are you okay?" I ask.

"My chest feels so tight...I can't seem to catch my breath..." she starts to break out in a cold sweat.

"She doesn't look so good," Matty says. Then suddenly grandma falls to the ground.

"Mom!" Dad comes running to his mom and he kneels down by her side. "Mom, can you hear me?"

"What's wrong with Nana?" Sara asks.

"Call 911!" Dad shouts.

My hands are shaking as I dial my phone.

"MOM!" Dad screams again. "She's stopped breathing."

I remember watching an episode of a TV show with my mom where they performed CPR on someone and they did it in time with an old song, *Staying Alive.*

I remember Mom sang along when we were watching. She wondered out loud if they would still use that song if it were called, *Staying Dead.* This is the crap that's going through my head. I hand my cell phone over to Matty and start pounding on Grandma's chest while singing, *"Ah, ah, ah, ah, stayin' alive..."*

I can't remember the lyrics, Mom jumps in and sings lead, as I pump Grandma's chest, *whether you're a brother or whether you're a mother...*

Still nothing.

Dad joins my mom sining, *you're stayin' alive, stayin' alive,*

I keep pumping Grandma's chest while my parents sing together,

feel the city breakin' and everybody shakin' stayin' stayin' aliiiiiiiveeeeee...

Suddenly, Grandma takes a gasp! Her eyes open.

"Wow," Matty says, punching my arm.

Sara claps. "Yay! Lauren saved Grandma!"

apprehension

*[ap-ri-**hen**-shuh n]*
anticipation of adversity or misfortune; suspicion or fear of future trouble or evil.

We're all in the hospital waiting room. No one's talking.

I wonder if anyone is not freaked out by hospitals.

Hopefully doctors and nurses aren't. Doctors and nurses must have an extra gene in them that keeps them immune to the misery of these places. Or they've developed such a strong tolerance that they remain unaffected. Or maybe some of them are affected, and when they go home from a day at work, they drown their sorrows in a tumbler of scotch and have horrible nightmares about the ones they couldn't save. I don't know how they deal, because the smell of death in the air in these places is throwing my good pal, OCD, into overdrive.

Two, four, six, nurses rushing by.

Two, fours, six, eight, ten anti-bacterial pumps in the hallway.

Two, four, people in wheelchairs.

One baby crying.

Yes, hospitals are also a place where people get better, but for some reason, I never dwell very long on that fact. My mind decides to marry itself to the death stat instead. My mind can be a real jerk sometimes.

Matty and Taylor are huddled close. They keep exchanging micro expressions of concern. Dad is pacing near the nurses' station and continuously makes eye contact with them so they don't forget about us. Mom is sitting perfectly still, staring at her hands.

"She's going to be okay," I tell her.

She continues to stare at her hands as if she's seeing them for the first time. "They don't look like my hands. These hands look like my mother's hands."

My mom's mom died when she was just thirteen. She rarely talks about her, but from the photos I've seen, they look a lot alike. Mom's mom had that sad distant look in her eyes that I've seen so many times in my mom's. I sometimes stand in front of the mirror to see if I can see it in my own face, too, but so far, it hasn't surfaced.

"I like your hands," I tell her as I reach for one. This brings her back to me.

She smiles sweetly, "Oh, Lauren. What will we do if she doesn't get better?"

"She will," I tell her.

"She's old. Old people die," she says.

"She's not that old, and some old people don't die until they're, you know, really, really, old."

Mom watches Dad as he paces. "Who will take care of him?" she wonders, "And who will take care of me?"

"Maybe you two can look after each other," I offer.

She looks at me the same way she was looking at her hands a moment ago. She strokes my hair. "And what about my Lauren? Sweet, sweet, Lauren. Who will take care of her?"

Sometimes my mom asks a question, and the question sounds more like she's blowing away a wispy cloud than a question that needs answering. So I don't answer.

I look up and catch my dad's eyes. They're glassy, holding onto a supply of tears that are waiting for the green light to travel down his face.

I tighten the grip on Mom's hand, get up, and we all approach the doctor. Matty and Taylor are right behind me.

"How is she?" Dad asks.

The doctors says, "She's suffered a minor myocardial infarction. Which is just another way of saying, she had a heart attack."

"And?" I ask.

"And she's going to be okay," the doctor says.

Geez, you think she would have led with that bit of information.

"Thank God," Dad says, hugging Mom.

I like seeing them hug like this. I wish it didn't take a near fatality to get here, but I guess we can't choose how things come into being.

"But," the doctor continues, "she will need to take it easy for a few weeks. You'll need to keep an eye on her stress levels, and no running around. And no more hiking."

We all make our way to Grandma's room. On that short walk, my first thought is…now I have another person to keep alive.

reclaim

{rə'klām}

to bring back to a preferable manner of living, sound principles, ideas.

It's been fifteen days since Grandma's minor myocardial infarction, and shockingly, she's been an okay patient. She hasn't tried moving any furniture around, plus I've made her a few meals, and she even complimented me on my baked zucchini muffins, telling me that the consistency was heavenly. That's right, she used the word "heavenly." I wouldn't lie about word usage.

"I got it," I say, intercepting Mom in the driveway. She's about to drive Dad to a meeting.

"No, sweetie. You go write. I can take him," she says.

"No, you go do something that you like. You never do anything you like." It occurs to me that I have no idea what my mom likes to do. And then I remember a framed drawing my dad hung in the garage. It's of a woman who looks like she's part angel, part animal. I asked him about it when I was a kid, and he told me that it was "one of Mom's drawings." He said it as if she had many. Mom never spoke of her drawings. Still, I take a stab at it.

"You like to draw."

"Oh. That."

"Don't you?"

"I did. Once."

"Can't you again?"

"I'm not very good."

"Yes, you are. I saw your drawing in the garage."

"Do you like it?" she asked.

"Yes. Very much."

She's pleased by this. Her shoulders relax. "Oh. Well, I suppose I can doodle some."

She hands me the car keys and walks back into the house. I approach the car, my dad's already in the passenger's seat.

"Lauren?" He's surprised. "Your mom said she'd drive me—"

"It's okay. I want to." I start the engine and begin to drive him to his meeting.

"I could just call a Lyft."

"You don't want me to take you?"

"It's not that, it's just…" His thoughts trail off as he looks out the window.

"It's just what?"

"Matty had a family meeting while you were away that day."

"I know. She told me. So?"

"So, she sat us all down and told us about everything you had to give up in order to take care of things after I left."

"It's okay, it's not a big deal."

"That's exactly what I told her," he says happily.

I didn't expect him to agree with me. Not before thanking me profusely, anyway.

"Yeah," he continues, "I told her that you could handle it because that's just how you are."

"You said that?"

"She said I was missing the point and yelled at me. But, I know my Sunflower loves to be in charge." He ruffles my hair. "Anyway, I promised Matty that I'd try to be more self-sufficient. That's why I suggested calling a Lyft. But, I mean, if you're good, then we're good."

I can't believe my little sis had to speak up for me.

I can't believe I don't speak up for myself.

I can't believe he thinks this is all not a big deal.

I pull the car over to the side of the road and shut off the engine.

"It's not for another few blocks—" Dad stops as soon as he sees the look on my face.

"Actually...it's not good."

"It isn't?"

"No, it isn't. And it IS a big deal. It's a big, fucking deal."

"Whoa, Lauren, hold on—"

"I'm done holding on! There will be no more holding on. No more holding onto this fractured family, to your needs and Mom's needs and now your mom's needs-everybody needs something, right? *Everybody. Well, I'm an everybody too!"*

My dad is stunned into silence.

I take a deep breath and calmly start the engine.

My eyes are on the road, but I can feel him looking at me. I don't say anything. After a few moments, I can hear him, too...

I glance over to see him weeping. Again. Actors are so damn emotional. Still, it's a sad sight to see and I do feel badly.

I think of Carlie.

I think of YouTube Harmony.

And then I remind myself, once again, that all things are temporary.

I keep my eyes on the road and wait for this to pass, as I listen to the sounds of my father's regrets fill up the silence between us.

Why do you, why do you, why do you, why?
If only I could just
crawl inside of your mind
and know it entirely by proximity.
I wouldn't have to
ask questions,
solve puzzles,
wonder,
wander.
I could absorb all that is you,
just by being near.
and all questions,
would be answered.
and all questions,
would be silenced.
and all questions,
wouldn't matter anymore.
I would simply,
easily,
effortlessly,
just,
know.
I would lay back inside of your mind and gaze up
at the stars, finally free from the constant noise of,
Why do you,

Annie Wood

why do you,
why do you,
why?

abdicate

[ab-di-keyt]
to give up or renounce.

Text from Enzo:

> *wanna hook up?* 🏆

Text to Enzo:

> *I do not.*

hullabaloo

[huhl-uh-buh-loo]
a clamorous noise. an uproar.

"I'm in! I'm in!" I scream, rushing into the kitchen holding up my laptop.

Mom looks up from her coffee.

"In what, honey?"

Matty takes off her headphones. "What's going on?" Sara comes bouncing over. "Did we win a prize?"

"The writer's retreat! I've been accepted!"

Mom beams. "Oh. I knew it. I just knew it."

Grandma and Dad come in from the living room. "What's all the fuss about?"

"Sit." I say as I pull out two chairs around the kitchen table.

I clear my throat and read the email out loud.

"Dear Lauren Brighton,

It is with great pleasure we are writing to inform you of your acceptance into The Write Stuff writing retreat. Your work shows great promise. We look forward to working with you."

It's finally happening.
My life is finally calling.
And I'm finally ready to answer.

Now is the time to rewrite your life.
Before someone else starts scribbling all over the
pages of you.
Before you forget the plot,
The time,
The place.
Now is the time to rewrite your life.
The first draft was lopsided.
The second will be better.
Start right now.
Even if you don't know the meaning.
Even if you don't know how it ends.
Now is the time to rewrite your life.
And this time,
you're the one
playing the lead.

enterprise

[en-ter-prahyz]
a project undertaken or to be undertaken, especially one that is important or difficult, or that requires boldness or energy.

The car is packed up with all my earthly goods. The fellowship is in Santa Barbara, which is just two hours away, but I'm hoping to not need to come back for anything anytime soon.

All of us are standing in the driveway, gearing up for our grand goodbyes like the last scene of a movie where all the characters want to say the most perfect thing, but the pressure of the moment must have gotten the best of everyone, because we all just stand there with our hands in our pockets, swaying side to side, saying nothing at all.

Finally, Mom breaks the silence. "I made you a grilled cheese sandwich and I packed an apple and some of those mozzarella slices you like and a cup of iced raspberry green tea." She hands me the bag of food and the tea.

"Thanks, Mom. Oh, don't forget, once school starts, Matty needs extra help with math and Sara's starting a new school so she might be fussy at first…"

"Yes, yes, don't worry. I'm here. We all are," Dad says.

"And if Mom doesn't leave her room before noon, or if you can't find her at night—"

Mom swoops at me and kisses the tip of my nose. "Mom is fine."

"But, not really. I mean, not entirely, you know?" I tell her, carefully.

"No, not entirely. But, we're working on it," she says.

I turn to Grandma. "He should go to at least three meetings a week, more if possible."

Mom grabs me and pulls me in closely. She hugs me and whispers in my ear, "Sweet, sweet, Lauren. It's time for you to let go."

She pulls me away from her and looks tenderly, at me so tenderly I could cry.

"Just a little bit. Okay?" she adds.

"Okay," I say. And I want to. I really want to.

"I miss you sooooo much!" Sara screams.

"But I haven't even left yet," I say.

"I got a head start!" Sara says.

Everyone laughs, and the air seems to be circulating normally around us once again.

"You be good," I tell Sara. "I'm always good."

"Okay. Then be less good."

"Really?"

"No. Just…be you," I tell her kissing her head.

Matty comes over somewhat awkwardly. "So, I'll text and everything, to, you know, keep you updated and whatever," she says.

"That would be great. Thanks, Matty."

"Sure," she says.

"Can I ask you something?"

"Yeah?"

"Why did you hit submit?"

"Just in case you…" She pauses and I think she's going to tell me what we both know—that there was a chance that I would have talked myself into not leaving. But instead she finishes with, "In case you forgot to do it. You've been so busy, you know?"

I hug my sister tightly and she doesn't pull away. In fact, she actually hugs me back.

"I love you, Matty."

"I know. I love you, too, bossy-butt."

And with that, holding back tears, I say my last I love yous and goodbyes as I quickly hop into the car, and drive away. I look into the rearview mirror and watch my complicated, loving, bizarre family get smaller.

And smaller.

And smaller.

Until they all,

completely,

disappear.

I adjust my focus on the open road ahead, where anything is possible.

***

I've been driving for an hour and half with the windows rolled down and the music blaring. I sing along, not even caring about my tone deafness. I was singing for joy, not for show. Zooming up the 101, I've never felt so much like me. I'm flying high. These past ninety minutes have been some of my all-time favorite minutes.

I pull over to make a pit stop at a gas station in Ventura County to use the bathroom. Mom's green tea grande was a bit too grande and I have to pee like a race horse.

I first notice him by the Sun Chips. His dirty blonde, wavy hair is shoulder length, giving him a total Cali surfer boy vibe. But he wears glasses, which make him look more like a nerdy surfer. He's tall and skinny and he's wearing a t-shirt with the image of *The Little Prince* on it.

I think I'm in love.

When he catches me looking, he smiles shyly and then turns away. I really, really, really have to pee, but I'm worried that nerdy-surfer boy won't still be standing there by the Sun Chips when I return. So, I "girl up" and hold my pee in. Then I do something I've never done before. I make the first move.

"Hi, I'm Lauren."

He looks up.

"Hi. Matthew."

"I like your shirt."

"Thanks. It's my favorite book."

"Mine, too."

"Cool."

His sweet smile makes me momentarily forget about the green tea grande creating a tsunami in my bladder. "Do you live in Ventura?" I ask him.

"No, I'm from San Diego. But, I'm moving to Santa Barbara for school."

"Me, too. I'm going to The Write Stuff writing re-treat," I tell him proudly.

"You're a writer?" he asks.

I take a moment. A short moment. And then I real-ize... "Yes. I am. I am a writer."

"The Write Stuff? I've heard about that place. That's supposed to be super hard to get into. You must be good," he says. "I paint," he says, abstracts mostly."

"That's cool."

"Yeah. Gotta create, right?" He smiles.

...And so I don't create a pool on the floor of the 7-Eleven, I excuse myself.

"I really have to...it was nice meeting you, Mat-thew." I rush off to the bathroom, cursing myself for drinking that stupid green tea.

"Nice to meet you, too," he yells back.

When I return from the restroom, I look up and down every aisle for Matthew, but he's nowhere to be found. Why didn't I ask him to wait? I should have asked him to wait!

I am so pissed at my bladder right now. No pun intended.

I mean, I'm kind of pleased with myself for start-ing the conversation in the first place, but I really should have planned it out better. I need to work on my follow-through.

Maybe I should've asked for his number or asked him what street he lives on. But what about him? He couldn't have waited three minutes for a girl to take a quick pee?

Okay, the new and improved me is not going to beat myself up about this. I took a chance, and sometimes when you take a chance, things still don't work out the way you want, and that's just…life. It's still good that I took a chance. Now, on to more important things. Off to my future. *Remember, Lauren, your life is not all about a stupid boy, anyway.*

Only, he's not stupid. He reads. He paints. He loves *The Little Prince.*

Focus, Lauren, focus.

I hop into the car and resume my drive. I turn up the volume and get lost with abandon on the open road.

Before I know it, someone is honking at me. Rude. Honking should only be used to alert someone of something dangerous. I look around. It's Sun Chips Little Prince Matthew, pulling up alongside me.

Honking should also happen when a cute boy wants to get your attention.

"Matthew!" I say more gleefully than intended.

"Your number!" he yells. "Follow me!"

We pull over.

We get out of our cars and I give him my number. He puts it in his phone and then texts me.

may I take u 2 dinner 2morrow nite? 📷

I don't make him wait for my reply.

Yes.

He walks back to his car and as I make my way back to my car, I get an impulse. Not my normal impulses, like to count cars out of nervousness or avoid stepping on cracks out of superstition, but to do something else entirely.

I begin to whirl.

Right there on the side of the road, with the new boy watching, or not watching, I don't care…I just suddenly feel the need to…whirl.

So I whirl.

And I whirl.

And I can feel the joy of everything building up inside me—in this moment.

I whirl for who I've been.

I whirl for who I might become.

I whirl toward my future—toward the unknown, the imperfections, the messiness of it all.

I whirl for my desire to create something in the world.

Nothing needs fixing inside of this whirl.

I think of my family. I don't know how things will turn out for them, and I don't know what my life has planned for me.

But, here, in the freedom of this moment, inside this brand new whirl, there's a few things that I do know for sure:

My life…

It will be real.

It will be true.

And it will be

mine.

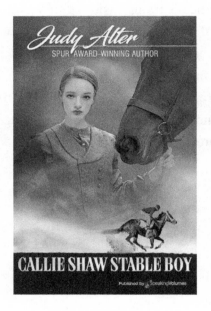

Sign up for free and bargain books

Join the Speaking Volumes mailing list

Text

ILOVEBOOKS

to 22828 **to get started.**